## SHE LOOKED UP
## AND THEIR EYES MET...

He had come up behind her, settled his hands over her towel-covered shoulders and turned her around. Amy knew there was something she wanted to say, but didn't know what it was. She felt breathlessly dizzy as she looked up, and completely adrift. What was she doing? What did she want to be doing?

He lowered his lips and touched them to hers. It was the lightest touch, velvet soft and warm. It was lovely...

# THE FORTUNE
# HUNTER

## Other Regency Romances from Avon Books

# THE FORTUNE HUNTER

## JO BEVERLEY

AVON BOOKS ◆ NEW YORK

AVON BOOKS
A division of
The Hearst Corporation
1350 Avenue of the Americas
New York, New York 10019

Copyright © 1991 by Jo Beverley
Published by arrangement with Walker and Company
Library of Congress Catalog Card Number: 91-13118
ISBN: 0-380-71771-9

First Avon Books Printing: December 1992

AVON TRADEMARK REG. U.S. PAT. OFF. AND IN OTHER COUNTRIES, MARCA REGISTRADA, HECHO EN U.S.A.

Printed in the U.S.A.

RA   10   9   8   7   6   5   4   3   2   1

# Author's Note

THE LONDON SEASON is often central to a Regency romance. Just think how central it was to many Regency people.

The landowning gentry and aristocracy spent most of their year at their estates. Their lives were tied up with country matters and their social lives revolved around the small number of upper-class families living nearby. (In terms of casual visiting, which was often on foot for ladies, a few miles would be the outer limit.)

If they were fortunate, these neighbors included people they liked, but it was quite likely that some of the small circle drove them crazy and they couldn't wait to see new faces and hear new jokes.

There was also the question of forming acceptable and congenial alliances. If the country gentry lived near a town, there would be assemblies drawing attendance from a wide area; meeting potential husbands and wives would then be less difficult. If they were more isolated, it could be that there was no single person of an appropriate age living nearby. Certainly the chance of finding one who was appealing was not as great as in a place were there was some selection.

The London Season did not originate, however, as a social function. It grew up around the sittings of Parliament. All the males of the peerage were members of Parliament for they were members of the House of Lords. Most of the gentry had at least one family member in the House of Commons because most families controlled an electoral district—a pocket borough.

Thus for generations many of the men had been making the journey up to London to attend the sittings of the Houses and protect their interests. This generally meant two visits—one in late autumn, one in late spring. They doubtless had a wonderful time, meeting together in the coffee houses and clubs, but it wasn't until the ladies became widely involved that the Season really began.

It was communication that created the Season. I had a history teacher who said that communication was the central fact of history, and she may well have been correct.

Before the mid-eighteenth century, English roads were the responsibility of the local boroughs, who largely failed to put in the work and money necessary to maintain them. They were quagmires in the rain, and frost or drought turned them into rock-hard ruts. Only the desperate took a carriage along these highways. Most preferred to ride. To add to the problem, coach springs were primitive and even a tolerable road did not give a comfortable ride.

In the mid-eighteenth century the turnpike system began to develop. Accordingly, trustees were given responsibility to improve and maintain roads and charge tolls to cover the cost. By the early nineteenth century there were thousands of toll booths and reasonably good roads throughout England.

This—along with the development of better road-surfacing materials by Telford and McAdam, and the invention of better vehicle spring suspension—led to a revolution in transportation in the early nineteenth century which seemed miraculous to people back then. They could at last take joy in travel.

Wives and families began to make the journey to London with their husbands. A social system was developed to suit their needs. It involved more than the balls and routs where alliances—political and marital—were made. It was also practical, cultural, and educational.

Remember that these often very sophisticated and

well-educated people were deprived in the country. They might receive a newspaper—days late. They could subscribe to various monthly magazines. They could, and did, write and receive letters. But that was it.

When they arrived in London they were at the center of the world. Here they heard the news as soon as the Regent heard it, often as it happened, for a great deal of the news happened in London.

Here they could see the latest fashions, furnishings, lighting, polishes, stoves, garden implements, farming equipment, stable goods, medicines, etc. The best of these would be taken back to improve life in the country.

Here they could talk to scholars, travelers, great scientists, and inventors. They could feed hungry minds and learn about the latest discoveries, such as steam power, laughing gas, and other things that were going to affect their daily lives, for this was a time of change.

Because London was the center of the world, interesting people gravitated to it. Consider the people one could meet in the relatively small world of Regency London: in the arts Constable, Turner, Lawrence, Fuseli, and Blake; in literature Southey, Wordsworth, Coleridge, Scott, Byron, Shelley, Keats, Lamb, Austen, Edgeworth, and Sheridan; in the sciences Davy, Faraday, Watt, Stephenson, and Jenner; in public life Wellington, Pitt, and Captain Bligh of the *Bounty*.

What a dinner party one could gather. And they did, they did. So let us not forget that there was more to the London Season than gambling, dandies, and parties, parties, parties.

I enjoy hearing from my readers. Please write to me care of the publisher and enclose an SASE for a reply. (U.S. stamps are fine.)

# THE FORTUNE HUNTER

# = 1 =

IT WAS A MERRY party in the kitchen of Stonycourt in Lincolnshire, seat of the de Lacy family. For once a generous fire was roaring in the grate, a chicken had been sacrificed to make a feast, and the precious store of medicinal spirits had been raided to make a fiery punch. The four young de Lacys and their aunt sat around the scrubbed deal table toasting their good fortune and making grand plans for the use of their newfound wealth.

Stonycourt's two remaining servants—aged specimens—hunched on a high-backed settle close to the fire like two black crows, nursing mugs of hot punch but casting a jaundiced eye on the jubilation.

"A horse!" declared Sir Jasper de Lacy, youngest of the family and yet nominal head. "A hunter. A prime bit of blood and bone."

"New gowns," put in his twin sister, Jacinth, with a blissful smile. "Bang up to the mark and *not* homemade."

At sixteen, the twins were still very alike, for Jasper was of a slender build, fine boned for a boy, and Jacinth had insisted in following fashion by having her curly brown hair cropped short. She had declared that it was the only fashionable gesture that came free.

"A Season?" offered the eldest daughter, Beryl. She added, in the tone of one who speculates on fabulous wonders, "Almack's?"

Amy de Lacy, the middle daughter, smiled sadly. Beryl was one who dreamed of wonders, but always with a

1

question mark after them. In truth, life had not served to raise Beryl's expectations. Though she had a sweet nature and a great many useful skills, no one could deny that she was plain—the sort of lumpy, sallow homeliness which could not be disguised by discreet paint or a stylish haircut.

As the daughter of Sir Digby de Lacy of Stonycourt and with a portion to match, Beryl could have expected to marry. That had all gone up in smoke two years ago when their father died and the tangle of bills and borrowings which had supported them in elegance had come crashing down.

Amy had suffered on her own behalf, for it was not at all pleasant to be poor, but she grieved more for Beryl, who was the kind of woman who should marry and have a home and children and now, doubtless, would not. Beryl was kind, skillful, and endlessly patient. She would make an excellent mother and she deserved a good, prosperous man to make her dreams come true.

"That's right," said the older lady seated at the head of the table, merrily tipsy beneath a tilted blue satin turban. "That's what's needed, Beryl pet. A Season. It'll be grand to be back in London, especially now peace is in the air. We'll soon have you married, then Amethyst, then Jacinth."

Amy winced. She had persuaded everyone else in the world to give up her ridiculous name in favor of Amy, but Aunt Lizzie would not be moved. "My dear sister chose your name with loving care, Amethyst," she would protest, "and I will not betray her now she is in her grave." Put like that it made a simple change of name sound like a heinous sin.

But since Georgiana de Lacy had taken it into her head to call all her children after precious stones, why could Amy not have been Agate or Onyx? Or Sardonyx. Yes, she'd rather have liked being Sardonyx de Lacy.

But she would much rather have been called Jane.

She also wished Aunt Lizzie would not encourage the family tendency to flights of fancy. What else was to be expected, however? It seemed to be a trait which ran strong on both sides of the family tree.

After all, Amy's maternal grandparents—prosperous London wine merchants—had named their daughters Georgiana and Elizabeth after the famous Gunning sisters, clearly with social advancement in mind. In fact, they had achieved mild success. Lizzie had not married, but the beautiful Georgiana had married Sir Digby de Lacy of Stonycourt.

It was a shame, thought Amy, that this had so dizzied the Toombs family that they had sunk into penury trying to live up to their daughter's social heights. Some prosperous relatives would be very useful these days.

The trait of impracticality was strong on the paternal side, too. Amy's father had been a devout optimist and so delighted with his beautiful bride that he had been unable to deny her anything. He had extended his indulgence to each child without thought to his resources. They had been so happy, thought Amy wistfully, and the lovely house had frequently been full of guests and had rung with laughter.

She would give anything to have those days back.

"I don't think I would care for a Season really," Beryl demurred, coloring. "I'm a little old to be making my curtsy. . . ."

"Nonsense, pet," said Lizzie. "What do you say, Amethyst?"

Above all, Amy hated being faced with the choice of supporting these bubbles of fancy or exploding them. The truth was that Beryl was too old, and that, plain as she was, the chance of her making a match in London was slim indeed, but how could she say that? It wasn't as if Jasper's share in a winning lottery could support such an enterprise anyway, and she could still wring his neck for risking his hard-won book money on such an idiotic enterprise.

Everyone was waiting for her answer and so she said carefully, "I fear there simply isn't enough money. It's a drop in the ocean."

Dismay wiped away joy. Lizzie opened her mouth but it was Jacinth who got in first. "Amethyst de Lacy," she burst out, the use of the full name a protest in itself, "if you are going to be a wet blanket, I swear I will hate you forever!"

Amy pulled an apologetic face. "I'm sorry, Jassy, but we have to be sensible."

"*Why?*" demanded Jasper. "Look what sensible has achieved. We've been holed up here for two years like . . . like troglodytes, living from hand to mouth. No hunting. No dancing. No fun at all! It's only when I go and do something *unsensible* that we get anywhere!"

"Fine," snapped Amy. "And how are you going to build on this? Spend it all on *more* lottery tickets? Or perhaps you'd rather take it to the races?"

Jasper reddened. "I do seem to have a winning streak." At his sister's groan, he quickly added, "But there's no need for that. We have *five thousand pounds!*"

Jacinth cheered and offered another toast. Amy feared her little sister was on the go.

"Jasper," Amy said gently but firmly, "your masters say you are very good with figures. How many hunters will the income from the money buy and keep? How many fine outfits? How many Seasons will it provide at the same time as it keeps up Stonycourt?"

"To hell with Stonycourt."

Aunt Lizzie gasped. "Jasper!"

"Sorry," he muttered. "But, Amy, the money will buy a lot."

"Not if you preserve the capital. If you can invest it to produce three hundred a year you will be doing well. That will provide a modicum of comfort but you should use some of it to pay down the encumbrances on the estate." Amy sought for a more cheerful aspect. "Of course, if you apply it all to the debt, then it will mean less time until it is cleared. Once we have paid all the debts, you can use the rents for income. We can slowly build."

"Slowly!" Jacinth burst out. "Slowly. That's what you always say. What about poor Beryl? She's twenty-three! She can't wait."

Beryl smiled sadly. "Don't you worry about me, Jassy. I know I'm not going to find a husband without a dowry, and this money can't provide one. Amy's right," she said with a sigh. "I'm afraid we're all going to be spinsters."

Jacinth looked aghast at this. She had obviously never previously applied the family's straightened circumstances to herself. "Not Amy," she declared spitefully. "She has only to stand on a corner of the highway to have men groveling at her feet!"

The moment the words were out she looked appalled, clapped a hand over her mouth, and then fled the table with a wail. Jasper scowled accusingly at Amy, then leapt up to go after his twin. Lizzie clucked and heaved herself up to follow.

Beryl placed a comforting hand over Amy's. "She didn't mean it."

Amy squeezed that hand but she said, "Yes, she did, and it's true. I wish to heaven I was plain as a barn door."

For Amy had the curse—as she saw it—of stunning beauty. Her hair was a glittering blond of such complexity of hue that the swains who regularly compared it to spun gold were not being as trite as it would appear. Her face was a charming heart shape; her nose straight but slightly upturned; her soft full lips were a perfect Cupid's bow, curved so that it was extremely difficult for her not to appear to be smiling. Her eyes were large and of a subtle dark blue lightened by flashes of lighter shades like a stream in the sun. Her skin, despite much time out of doors, was flawless.

Amy was just tall enough to be called elegant, and her form was sweetly rounded with a tendency to lushness in the upper part, which she particularly deplored.

Amy had never been at ease with her beauty, for it seemed to make people behave in very silly ways—men ogled and clustered, and women were frequently acidic—but she had borne it until the family's plunge into poverty. Then she had realized how it set her apart from her sisters, just as Jassy had said. Amy would always find a husband if she sought one, whereas Beryl—much more worthy of love—was unlikely to, and even Jassy, pretty as she was, might fail without a penny to her name.

So Amy had spent the last two years doing her best to obliterate her beauty. She had always had a taste for simple garments, and after her father's death she had stripped them of all trimmings and dyed the brighter ones into dull colors. Mourning had provided a good excuse, and those which had survived the black dye vat had been plunged into a brown one, with the explanation that it made them more suitable for work.

"But Amy, dear," Beryl had said, "I cannot see why a brown dress is more practical than a pink one unless you mean that it will not look dirty when it is. I do not like that thought at all."

Amy had had no satisfactory response to that one.

She had used the same excuse, however—their new need to do the work once done by a dozen servants—to take to wearing her hair scraped back into a tight knot and covered by a cap. Beryl had found no logical argument against that, except that it was not very becoming.

Amy had hoped she was right, but neither clothes nor cap seemed to reduce Amy's quantity of admirers, and Amy wanted them reduced to zero, for she could not bear to marry while her sisters were left spinsters.

In desperation, she had made the experiment of having her hair cropped short like Jacinth's. That had been a disaster, and she was waiting impatiently for it to grow. For the moment there was no question of confining it at all. It rioted around her head like a cherub's curls, emphasizing not just her beauty but a childlike impression she abhorred.

"If you were as plain as a barn door," said Beryl with a teasing smile, "it would be even harder on us, dearest. I enjoy seeing your beauty."

Amy squeezed Beryl's hand again, touched by the sincere words. Beryl had no scrap of envy in her. "But perhaps I am too serious-minded," she said. "Since we never expected to have this money, it would do no harm to spend it on fripperies."

"It would do no good either," said Beryl, "except develop a taste for more. I'm sure you were right when you said it would be better to live very simply for a few years so that Stonycourt be restored." She did not sound very sure.

"You are the oldest," said Amy. "If you think we should manage in a different way, please say so."

"Oh no," said Beryl honestly. "I have no notion at all. Left to myself, I suppose I would have carried on as Papa did, had it been possible to get credit. I am good at finding ways to manage on less, but I can't plan as you do, and figure out our finances, and how long it will take . . . it would all be too depressing." She worried a groove in the table with her fingernail, then asked, "How long will it take, Amy?"

Amy had done her best to be vague on such matters, and in typical fashion, the family had not pressed her, but she would not shrink a straight question. "Four years," she said, "if we're very careful, and rents stay high, and there is no disaster such as the roof leaking. . . ." She stopped herself from listing all the unexpected expenses which could arise to throw her calculations into chaos. "In four years," she said cheerfully, "we should be almost free of debt, and Jasper's income will be adequate for Stonycourt to become a proper home again."

"That will be pleasant for Jasper," Beryl said, "but what of us?"

Amy felt as if a void had opened at her feet. In all her plans and calculations, she had never looked further than her cherished goal—to restore Stonycourt to the way it had been before their world fell apart. "We will live here," she said uncertainly. "There may even be a small amount for marriage portions."

But Beryl would be twenty-seven by then. Amy was suddenly aware that Jacinth was right. Beryl couldn't wait. "Perhaps we are holding too tight," she said. "We could reconsider selling some land and put the money aside for dowries. Uncle Clarence would approve that. He said as much."

Uncle Clarence was their guardian, though he lived in Cumberland and paid little heed to their affairs.

"Oh no," said Beryl firmly. "We agreed it would be disastrous to begin selling off the land. Four years is not so long." She sighed. "I do wish we could have some real tea, though." She went over to the stove and spooned dried chamomile into the pot.

Amy would have chopped her own heart and put it in the pot if there'd been any purpose to it. "A pound of tea would make a tiny dent in five thousand pounds, love," she said.

Beryl shook her head. "And gowns for Jassy, and a horse for Jasper. No, let's stick to our guns."

Jacinth came back, accompanied by Jasper and Lizzie. "Oh Amy, I'm sorry," she said with a sniff. "That was a horridly catty thing to say."

Amy went over and hugged her. "Don't regard it, love. The only blessing of having this phiz is that *I* don't have to look at it all day. I'm sure it's very wearing. But you see, don't you, that we have to be careful for a little longer so Stonycourt can be Stonycourt again."

Jasper looked mutinous. "I don't think everyone's happiness should be sacrificed to a building."

"It's the home of the de Lacys, dear. We can't let it go, or fall down about our ears."

Beryl brought the teapot to the table. "Amy's right. But I think we should plan for what we are to do when everything is straight again. Jasper will want to marry, and his bride won't want a house full of spinsters."

Amy was touched by this sudden attack of practical thinking and disturbed yet again. Her faith in her own clearheadedness was being rapidly undermined. First she had assumed they would all be marriageable when their fortunes were stable again, then she had assumed they would all live on here happily as they had once done.

"I don't want to marry anyway," said Jasper nobly.

Beryl smiled gently. "Think of the succession, dear."

He went bright red. "Oh, true."

Jacinth looked resentfully at her twin. "But *I* want to

marry. And what's to become of us if we don't? I won't become a governess or a companion. I won't."

Beryl poured her some tea and reverted to form. "You must look on the bright side, Jassy. It could all work out for the best. If you do have to seek employment, you and Amy are sure to attract the attention of the sons of the house and end up rich."

Amy shut her eyes. Such an adventure was one of her recurrent nightmares but the outcome would not be as benign as Beryl imagined. Since their poverty had become known Amy had received a number of sly propositions.

"I'm sure that would be very nice," said Aunt Lizzie doubtfully. Amy thought for a moment that her aunt was for once going to point out a folly, but she carried on. "I agree with Jacinth. Employment would not be at all pleasant and not at all necessary. A thousand pounds to each of us would be enough for us to live quietly in a cottage. Less if we all live together." There was a loud clearing of throats from the settle near the fire.

The two old servants, Mr. and Mrs. Pretty, had been butler and housekeeper at Stonycourt for thirty years, and when disaster struck they had been too old to seek employment elsewhere. When the other staff had been let go, they had stayed on, accepting room and board, waiting for the pension to which they felt they were entitled.

To which they were entitled, admitted Amy, even if Sir Digby had neglected such provisions. Lizzie Toombs looked sourly at the couple but said grudgingly, "And doubtless a thousand for the Prettys. The estate should be able to bear that, and if Jasper marries an heiress we'll all be well set."

"No, we won't!" cried Jacinth. "We'll be growing old in a cottage!" She looked around the table for reassurance. When it did not come, she burst into tears and fled again.

"What's the matter with her?" asked Jasper blankly. "If I did marry an heiress I'd see Jassy all right."

"I'm afraid that will be a while dear," said Amy. "I

doubt you'll be able to marry a fortune for a good many years."

"Oh. Well then," he said carelessly, "I think *you* should. With your looks, you should be able to snaffle a duke as easy as falling off a chair."

There was silence. Then, "Of course," said Aunt Lizzie blithely. "What a clever young man you are, Jasper. We will use the money to take Amethyst to London. She'll be the toast of the town and marry a duke and we'll all be rich."

Amy felt as if she couldn't breathe. It must be the punch. "But what about Beryl?" she protested, the first defense she could think of. "The eldest should marry first."

Beryl laughed. "I couldn't catch a duke, dear. Nor would I want one. I will choose a husband with a small estate, a man who stays at home."

She was off in one of her dreams. As far as Beryl was concerned, "I will" was as good as done. Amy slapped her wits back into order. Was it possible? Marriage was a way out of poverty, after all, and she *would* do anything to make all right for her family.

"It would be madness to spend all the money," she said cautiously. "A thousand should be more than enough if we're careful. In fact," she added thoughtfully, "it may not be necessary to go to London at all. We live on the edge of the Shires, and it is still hunting season. There must be many wealthy gentlemen in this locality. As Jassy said," she added dryly, "I have only to be seen to slay."

"It would be much more fun to go to London," said Beryl simply.

Amy didn't have the heart to tell her it would be far to expensive for them all to go. Beryl's words merely stiffened her resolve to try other means. It would be perfectly horrid to be gadding about Town while Beryl and Jassy pined at home.

"If we are to do this," she said firmly, "we must remember that I will need to marry a very rich man, one willing to lay out a lot of money to bring the estate back into heart immediately and provide dowries for you and Jassy. I think on the whole I should look for an older man. A nabob, perhaps, or a wealthy cit."

"What!" declared Aunt Lizzie. "Marry beneath you when your mother struggled to raise herself up."

"We are not so high now, Aunt," Amy pointed out.

"You are a de Lacy of Stonycourt."

Amy shrugged. "Let us hope that makes me worth extra at market."

"But a gentlemen who marries a golden dolly," said Beryl doubtfully, "raises her up to his status. A lady who marries a wealthy cit sinks down to his. I don't think you'd like that, Amy dear. You should marry the duke."

Amy shook her head. "If one offers," she said gently, "be sure I will consider him most seriously. But we must be practical. Money is our main object, accompanied by a generous disposition."

She summoned up a merry smile and raised her tea-cup. "To fortune hunting!"

Over the next days Amy marshaled her family like a general. Aunt Lizzie was set to writing to her acquaintance in London to discreetly enquire about rich tradesmen interested in marrying into the gentry. As Beryl had pointed out, such a marriage was not as popular as the linking of men of good birth with lower-bred fortunes, for it did not automatically raise a man up as it would a woman. But it did give useful connections, and the children could expect to step into the gentry if they'd a mind to, so it had some benefits to offer.

Jasper had returned to his school at Uppingham and was asking if there were any nabobs or such living in the nearby villages, here for the hunting. There was a degree of urgency to this. It was April and the hunting season was winding down as the crops began to grow. Soon all the wealthy Meltonians would be off to London.

Amy and her sisters took to paying especial attention to local gossip but were frustrated by the fact that all anyone wanted to talk about these days was Napoleon

Bonaparte's abdication. This wonderful news would normally have delighted them, but Amy at least wished the dramatic events could have delayed for a little while so that people would still be interested in the minutiae of local life.

April progressed without anything being achieved. Aunt Lizzie received only gossipy replies from London full of plans for victory celebrations but lacking lists of wealthy bachelors.

Jasper wrote that he discovered there were a goodly number of avid hunters still in the area but the single men were all young bucks, and though well-breeched enough none were rich enough for their purposes.

Beryl and Jassy mulled over the local residents with care but could not keep it in their minds that a veritable Croesus was required, and his looks or age were of no account.

"There's that charming Mr. Bunting over at Nether Hendon," said Beryl one evening as they ate their mutton stew. "He's tolerably handsome and I'm sure he has a sweet nature."

Amy forced a smile. "But if he has five thousand a year, I'd be surprised, Beryl."

"Five thousand a year is a comfortable income."

"But doesn't allow much for me to milk him of for Stonycourt," said Amy ruthlessly.

Beryl gaped. Aunt Lizzie frowned. "Amethyst, my dear, don't you think that was a little vulgar?"

Amy rested her head on one hand and gathered her patience. Then she looked up. "I'm sorry. It wasn't a proper thing to say. But there will be no point to this if I merely marry a man who will keep me in comfort. How could I live in comfort while my family suffers? So can we concentrate our efforts on finding another Golden Ball? Please?"

From the end of the table where they ate slightly apart from the family—by their own choice—Pretty cleared his throat.

"Yes, Pretty," Amy said.

"If I may be so bold, Miss Amethyst, I do know of a very rich man in this locality."

"Who?"

"There is a gentleman of the name of Staverley taken Prior's Grange in Upper Kennet. Talk down at the Jug and Whistle is that he is come from the West Indies very rich indeed and without wife or children that any knows of."

"Is he young?" asked Jassy excitedly.

"Is he handsome?" asked Beryl.

"Are we sure he's rich?" asked Amy.

"Anyone can be a trickster," said Pretty, "but it is the feeling of all that he's warm enough to toast with. Bringing in fine furniture, ordering all kinds of luxuries, hiring ample staff . . . and," he added with a slight sneer which revealed long stained teeth, "paying on the knob for everything."

"There's no need for that, Pretty," said Amy sharply. "We pay on the knob, too, these days. No one will give us credit. How do I meet this man?"

"Amethyst!" cried Aunt Lizzie. "Do not be so precipitate. We must make the most careful inquiries."

Amy opened her mouth to refute this but then closed it. It was clear that if anything practical was to achieved, she would be best advised to leave her family out of it. At least it seemed the Prettys could be relied on for help, even if it was only from self-interest. No bad thing, thought Amy. Self-interest could generally be relied on.

# ═ 2 ═

Two DAYS LATER Amy was on the road to Upper Kennet, driving the family's only vehicle—a dogcart—pulled by Zephyr, their only horse. Perhaps Zephyr had once been an appropriate name for this broken-down animal, but no more. She had only been kept because there'd be little profit in selling her.

As the horse plodded along, Amy told herself not to be so ungrateful. They were fortunate to have a beast to pull the old cart when needed, and though Zephyr was old and slow she was steady and willing. Clop, clop, clop went the hooves along the road. Amy let the ribbons lie slack as she reviewed her plan, searching out flaws.

Investigation had failed to discover a reliable way of meeting Mr. Owen Staverley. According to Pretty he was past forty, of a stocky build and a taciturn manner. It was said he walked with a limp, but there was no report of other ill health. He occasionally went into Oakham or as far as Lincoln on business, but apart from that he stayed at home. Whatever had brought him to this locality, it wasn't the hunting, for he kept only a carriage pair and a quiet hack.

Having failed to discover a public place where she could "accidentally" encounter him, Amy had decided on a cruder but simpler course. She was going to have an accident outside his gates. To this end she had frayed Zephyr's reins close to the bit so that at a sharp tug they would break. The tack was in such a worn-out state that no would ever suspect the damage to have been contrived. Of course, it would be clear to anyone with wits Zephyr needed no reins to control her, but Amy was willing to play the feebleminded wigeon if it suited her purpose. For once, her looks would be an advantage since they seemed to convince people she hadn't a wit in her head anyway.

She had told her family nothing of her plan in case they thought of some way to interfere. She was supposed to pick up some new laying hens from Crossroads Farm just beyond Upper Kennet. Five miles to get hens was not as outlandish as it appeared, for Mrs. Cranby had been the Stonycourt nursery nurse and could be depended on to give them good birds at a low price.

A sudden gust of wind swirled around and made Amy shiver. She looked up and found the sky was darkening. It had been a clear day when she set out, but it had taken two hours to get this far. Walking would have been faster, and if it was going to come on to rain she could perhaps have sought shelter at Prior's Grange without needing an accident of any sort. She told herself that a shower would make her piteous plight more touching, and a horse problem was more likely to engage the interest of the master of the house.

After all, it was not enough just to be given aid and shelter at the Grange; she needed to meet Mr. Staverley.

To avoid the possibility of being taken for a servant, Amy had dressed as well as possible. Since it was her business to attract, she had borrowed a gown and bonnet from Beryl—without, unfortunately, being able to ask her sister's permission. The outfit was not in the latest style, but it had been made three years ago by the best dressmaker in Lincoln, and the quality showed still.

The cambric gown was in a clear shade of blue, worked with a white stripe design. It played up Amy's coloring well. The high-crown bonnet was lined with matching blue silk and trimmed with white roses and a plume. The plume kept tickling Amy's cheek and was the devil of a nuisance.

Amy blew the feathers out of her eyes and glanced at the sky again. Though a little rain would be useful to her plot, a downpour would be unpleasant and ruin all this borrowed finery. She reached behind to investigate the box under the backseat, looking for any kind of protection. She was rewarded by two musty old sacks and a moth-eaten rug. Not much, but they would afford some protection.

The sky was definitely darker and the wind was picking up. Amy shivered and pulled the rug around her shoulders for warmth. If she hadn't been trying to catch a rich husband she would have her warm red woolen cloak with her and be less likely to catch her death instead. She'd always known romance was a stupid business.

How far to go? Another mile or so.

She picked up the reins and clicked to Zephyr to go faster. The horse didn't alter her pace at all.

"Come on, Zephyr!" Amy cried impatiently. "You can't be any keener on a soaking than I am."

Clop, clop, clop. Zephyr only had one pace.

Amy let the reins go limp again and settled to watching the sky and calculating their progress. She could see the rise of Upper Kennet in the distance.

The wind grew stronger, whipping up twigs and last year's leaves, swirling dust into Amy's eyes. Perhaps some got into Zephyr's eyes, for she tossed her head a little and her steady pace faltered. Amy grabbed the reins but the horse immediately steadied to her usual pace.

Amy took off the bonnet before the plume broke and placed it in the box. It would have some protection there, and now she could pull the rug close about her head. She certainly was going to be a piteous sight when she reached her target.

Then there was a flash of lightning and a crack of thunder. Not overhead but not far away either. "Oh, heavens," muttered Amy, grabbing the reins. The one thing likely to stir Zephyr to excitement was lightning. The old mare was probably too tired to create a fuss, but

Amy wished they were at Prior's George already. This was as much of a plight as she wished to be in.

She saw the rain coming. It swept over the fields toward her like a gray curtain, and when it hit it was sluicingly hard. Amy gasped and grabbed for the sacks to pull them on top of the rug over her head and shoulders. "Oh, poor Beryl's dress," she moaned.

Zephyr just dropped her head and plodded on.

There was a farmhouse of some sort on the right, with a light in a window. Amy thought of stopping to ask for shelter but she gathered up her courage. Just down this slight incline and up the next and she would be at the Grange. Now her situation was desperate enough to bring forward anyone's chivalrous instincts.

But the road had now become a stream. The wheels of the cart slipped one or twice, and Zephyr's pace faltered. A sign of uneasiness.

Suddenly a flash of lightning split the gray sky. It was followed almost immediately by a deafening crack of thunder. Zephyr stopped dead, then began to toss her head and back them toward the ditch. Amy grabbed the reins. "Ho! Steady, girl! Steady."

The horse responded and plunged forward. This surprising surge of energy almost sent them into the opposite hedge. Amy hauled back on the reins.

The reins broke.

Amy let out a very unladylike curse. She leapt from the seat and sloshed her way to grab the horse's head.

Zephyr immediately quieted and stood inert, head hanging. The rain poured down, and Amy was literally soaked to the skin. Another flash of lightning. Another roll of thunder. Zephyr twitched, but Amy's soothing voice and a comforting hand on her nose were enough for the weary mare.

Amy wished she had someone to comfort her. The noise and power of the rain were numbing her. Or perhaps it was just the cold. It hadn't seemed a cold day for late April, but now that she was wet she was chilled through.

In a moment we can go on, Amy thought.

The rain was slackening a little—going from torrent to downpour. She gathered her resources. It couldn't be more than a quarter mile to Upper Kennet, sanctuary, and a fortune.

Then the thinning of the rain showed her the road ahead. Though the slope of the road was very gentle, it formed a little dip before curving up to Upper Kennet. That dip was now a pond with two small rivers pouring into it. Prior's Grange was on the next rise, but it might as well be in India for all her chance of getting herself and the cart there today.

Amy muttered a few more distinctly unladylike words.

She considered wading through herself and making her way up to the Grange, but apart from the fact that she couldn't abandon poor Zephyr here, her behavior would appear strange enough to raise embarrassing questions. She would have to seek shelter at the farmhouse, and there was the devil of a chance of finding a rich husband there.

Amy could have wept from disappointment, weariness, and cold. She was shivering as she pushed and cajoled Zephyr into turning. Her hands were numb, her half-boots were up to their tops in muddy water. She eventually got the job done and tugged the horse wearily back the way they had come. The slope had seemed nothing as they had come down it; now it was a mountainside.

Surely it was only a minute since she had passed that flickering light. Where was it? Visions of a warm kitchen, hot tea, and dry clothing were dancing in her head.

There. A light.

It was a small, square farmhouse with a barn to one side and another outbuilding to the other. Surprisingly there were two open gates, one at either side. Amy simply picked the nearest.

Sensing shelter, Zephyr's pace picked up a little. She gave no trouble as Amy led her into the barn.

When the rain stopped beating down on Amy's head

it was a shocking relief. Amy leaned wearily against the horse's warm flank. She looked down. A dirty puddle was forming at her feet. Poor Beryl's dress.

She looked around. The storm had dimmed the day, but she could see this barn was rather ramshackle, probably unused. What sort of farm was this? She felt a trickle of unease at such evidence of neglect but stifled it. At least the barn was dry. The house would offer some kind of shelter.

Amy started to unharness the horse and rub her down, but her numb fingers were unable to perform the simple task. She blew on them, she tucked them into her relatively dry and warm armpits. It was no good, and her own shivering was getting worse by the minute. She could feel an impulse growing in her to burst into tears of misery. She had to get help.

She hated the thought of stepping out into the deluge, but across the muddy quagmire of a yard the warm golden light of a lamp glimmered in a window. She could see the shelves of a kitchen and could imagine the fire there, the warmth and aroma of the ovens. A haven.

Pointlessly, she dragged the soaked sacks further forward onto her face, then made a dash for it.

After three steps her feet went from under her. She slammed forward into the mud and slid for a yard or so. Stunned, she lay there winded. The mud was glutinously foul between her fingers. The rain beat down on her back. She could laugh or cry. She chose to laugh.

A fine beginning to her career as a fortune hunter. No one would want her at this moment.

It was tempting to just lie where she was, but Amy heaved herself up, her soaked muddy clothing like a millstone around her neck, and plodded carefully to the farmhouse door. It at least had a little porch covering it, and the rain stopped beating down on her head. She knocked. Nothing. She wiped her sodden hair back off her face with filthy fingers, picked up a stone, and beat on the door with that.

It swung open. Amy looked up to see a handsome,

tawny-haired young man in shirtsleeves staring at her in astonishment.

Harry Crisp had been congratulating himself on staying indoors on such a day. His friends, Chart Ashby and Terance Cornwallis, had ridden out early to ride with the Belvoir, unwilling to miss a day's hunting this close to the end of the season no matter how unpromising the weather. Served them right. They'd be drowned rats by the time they found shelter.

He doubtless would have been with them, however, if he hadn't felt the need for a bit of time to think.

At Easter he'd taken his usual trip to Hey Park, his family home. Chart disliked his parents and went home as little as possible, but Harry was fond of his. They were a good sort. They gave him an adequate allowance, and despite the fact that he was an only child, they didn't fuss over him, or try to interfere with his fun. His father was deeply suspicious of London and clearly feared Harry would one day be ruined there, but even so he made no cavil at Harry's annual jaunts there with Chart. Yes, a very good sort.

Moreover, Lord Thoresby was still under sixty and Harry had reckoned, when he'd thought about the matter at all, that he had many years before he need think of settling down.

Now he knew that his father was not well.

Lord Thoresby's untypical petulance about it had been alarmingly convincing. "Load of nonsense," he'd grumbled. "Just because I've been dizzy now and then."

"Perhaps I should come and help you here, sir."

"Rubbish! And miss the last of the hunting? None of that. I have people here to do what's needed."

"There's only a week or two left," Harry said. "Hardly worth going back for." His father looked as well as normal but he couldn't persuade himself this was all a mare's nest.

"Won't hear of it," said his father firmly. "In fact," he added a great deal less firmly, "I . . . er . . . I was thinking it's about time you spent more time in London."

Harry stared at his father in astonishment. "I can't think why."

Lord Thoresby rambled on about gaining a bit of bronze, learning to know a flat from a sharp, and a great many other unconvincing reasons. Harry took the puzzle to his mother.

"Oh dear," said Lady Thoresby. She was a small, plump, pretty woman who had given her son his tawny curls and amiable temperament. "I hoped he wouldn't . . . you mustn't mind him, Harry dear. He's a little out of curl these days. Don't like to feel he can't do just as he wishes."

"But why would he want me to go to Town?" Harry demanded. "I could understand if he wanted me home, and I'm more than willing."

"Marriage," said his mother apologetically. She looked at her horrified son and chuckled. "It is a state slightly better than hell on earth, dear one, but there is no need to hurry."

"He wants me to—Almack's?" Harry queried blankly.

"No doubt you'll enjoy it when the time comes," she assured him. "After all, a handsome young man, the heir to an old title and a substantial fortune, will suffer few rebuffs. But as I said, there is no need as yet. And you may meet a bride elsewhere." Lady Thoresby looked up from her needlework. "I hope you know, Harry, that your father and I would accept any bride of your choice. There is no need to look for a fortune, or grand connections. Just find a warmhearted girl, dear. One who will make you happy."

Harry allowed his mother's comfortable tone to reassure him. Perhaps it was time for him to start thinking about settling down, but not for a year or two. He was only twenty-four, after all.

But then his father suffered another dizzy spell, almost falling down the stairs. The doctor examined his patient again and shook his head. "No way to say, Mr. Crisp. He must build up his strength and avoid overexertion and excitement. He could be with us for many, many years." Silently he conveyed the grim alternative.

Lord Thoresby would not hear of Harry staying and became agitated on the matter, repeating his opinion that Harry should go to London. Marriage and nurseries were not mentioned but were clearly fretting Lord Thoresby's mind. Harry had returned to Rutland to arrange for the moving of his hunters and tell Chart what was afoot. His friend would doubtless be horrified.

Loosely connected on the family tree, and almost exactly of an age, they'd been inseparable since their first days at Eton. Harry couldn't imagine going bride-hunting without Chart, but it was a devil of a lot to ask of even the closest friend.

And a wife was likely to interfere with his normal masculine pursuits to an inconvenient degree.

As he mulled over these depressing thoughts, he was occupying his hands with his hobby and trying to mend a small automaton. The lady with china head and limbs and a blue silk gown was supposed to dance to the music box inside. She should point a toe, turn, and move her head. All she could manage was a jerky twitch.

He was poking beneath her silk skirts, grinning at the thought that this was rather improper, when he heard a thumping on the door. Who on earth would be out in such weather?

As he opened the door, rain and wind swept in and he was confronted by a mud creature. Sodden sacks for a head. Mud for a gown. The sacks moved and he saw a pale face.

"Good Lord." He opened the door farther and gestured for her to enter.

The woman, or girl—it was hard to say—staggered in, and he could shut out the noise and the cold, wet air. He looked blankly at his visitor and took in the growing pool of mud under her feet. Firkin, Corny's manservant, would have pungent words to say.

Consigning Firkin's future words to the devil, he said, "You must come into the kitchen." He directed the creature along the passage and into the warm room. Her shoes made slurping sounds as she plodded along.

Once in the room he looked at the trail behind her and said, "Er . . . perhaps you could shed some of your covering here."

Amy was coming back to some kind of sanity. She was still shivering cold and wetter than she'd been since she fell in the horse trough, but there was warmth about, and no wind, and no rain. "Who are you?" she asked the young man. He was clearly no farmer.

He gave her a small, elegant bow. "Harry Crisp, at your service, ma'am. You really should get out of those clothes. I'll find some towels and a blanket."

He turned away, and Amy said quickly, "You can't be alone here!"

"Can't I?" he asked with a raised brow. "Oh dear."

Amy didn't know what to do. "I can't possibly stay here alone with you," she said.

It occurred to Harry for the first time that this soggy mess spoke in the manner of a gentlewoman, and clearly a youngish one. It was a delicate situation. "Awkward, I grant you," he said. "But what else are you going to do?"

"I suppose," said Amy faintly, "I'd better go back to the barn and my horse." Her teeth started to chatter. Her nose was running. She sniffed.

"What good would that do?" he asked. "No one would know whether you'd been inside or out so why not stay in where it's warm and dry? You have a horse? Is it cared for?"

"N—no!" Amy wailed. "My hands were t—t—too c—cold!"

Harry had a strong urge to gather this waif in for a consoling hug, but apart from the mud, she'd doubtless set up a shriek of rape. "Don't worry about a thing," he said reassuringly. "Just wait a minute."

He ran up the narrow wooden stairs to the bedrooms and collected a stack of towels and a spare blanket. He didn't know whether the girl would have the wit to use them, but he'd do his best to see she didn't catch her death.

Back in the kitchen, she was standing as he had left her. He had the strange image of the mud drying and leaving her a grotesque brown statue in the kitchen of Coppice Farm. "Here ma'am," he said as he placed the pile on the table. "Make yourself as comfortable as you can, please. I'll go tend to your horse."

She didn't move. Harry shrugged. He didn't think he should strip her by force, though it might come to that if she was still fixed there when he returned.

He went into the passage, pulled on the heavy oil-skin cape which hung there, and plunged out into the downpour.

Amy heard his footsteps and the slap of the door as it closed behind him. She just stood there. To move seemed altogether too much trouble and she wasn't at all sure what was the right thing to do. But then something told her it was very bad to be standing here getting colder and colder with her teeth chattering. She moved toward the stove, which had a fire in the center. Her shoes went *squelch, squelch*. She looked behind at the muddy trail she was leaving and bit her lip.

She shed the sacks and rug, dropping them in a tidy pile in the corner. She stepped out of her shoes and abandoned them, too. She grabbed a towel and rubbed her face and hair, feeling the circulation coming back to her skin. But the rest of her was still so chilled.

As he had said, she needed to get out of all these sodden clothes. She couldn't! Then she sternly reminded herself that she was dedicated to pure reason. It made no sense to preserve her modesty at the cost of her life. But she had better do it quickly before her host returned.

She struggled her way out of her gown. She couldn't manage the lowest button with cold fingers, and so in the end she tore it free. The poor gown was done with anyway. That only left her shift and cotton stockings. The stockings were quickly done with and she rubbed her damp legs vigorously with the towel, gasping with pain and relief as the circulation began again.

She saw the way her wet shift clung to her legs and

24

giggled. Some dashing women were said to damp their skirts. She'd certainly gone to extremes in that regard. That reminded her that a young man was going to return at any moment and she was standing here as good as naked.

With a little cry she wrapped the blanket around her but it had scarcely touched her when she realized that it would only get wet from her wet shift. It might be her last bastion of modesty, but it would have to go.

She tore it off and frantically wrapped herself tentlike in the blanket. But that would never do. Her arms were imprisoned inside and if she moved, the whole thing gaped down the front. Ears straining for sound of her host's return, Amy wound the blanket around her body beneath her arms and tucked the end in securely. It was, she told herself, as decent as any gown except for her bare shoulders. She took up two of the small towels and tucked them down the back of her "gown," then crossed them over at the front and tucked the ends in under her arms like a fichu.

There was a small mirror on one wall and Amy peered into it. Her outfit actually looked very respectable. It wasn't of course, but it was the best she could do, and if her host was a villain it surely didn't matter what she was wearing.

She was still a mess. Though her hair was merely wet, her face was streaked with mud. She tried the pump at the sink and found it worked. She scrubbed at her face until it was clean.

Then she allowed herself to go over to the stove.

The warmth washed over her making her feel dizzy. There were two chairs there and Amy sank into one. She rested her feet on a convenient footstool close to the stove and held out her hands to the warmth, shuddering with the relief.

Hell might be pictured as flames, she thought, but this was surely heaven. She took a towel and rubbed at her hair, then tilted her head toward the heat. For once the crop was useful; it should dry in no time. As she ran her hands through it to speed the process, she looked around thoughtfully.

It was a very plain kitchen. There was the stone sink with the pump and a bucket underneath to catch the drainings. In the center of the room was a deal table and four chairs. To her right were the cupboards she had seen through the window, their contents hidden behind closed doors. Against the far wall stood a dresser with some pottery plates and cups upon it and three silver tankards. They struck her as strange in such a simple household.

But then her host did not belong in this place either.

It was not these things which struck her most, however, though she could not quite decide what did.

After a moment she realized. There was no aroma. She'd never before been in a kitchen without the smell of food. There was nothing cooking on the stove and, she would guess, hadn't been all day. There were no herbs hanging from the beams, no strings of onions and garlic.

The only sign of food at all was a loaf of bread on the table, along with a crock of butter and some cheese. Was that all her host ate? Perhaps he, too, was a victim of sudden poverty.

Amy became aware of hunger. She longed for some bread and cheese and a cup of hot tea.

There was a blackened kettle keeping warm to one side of the hob, but Amy had no way of knowing where the tea-making things were, if indeed the house could afford such a luxury. Besides, it would be overbold to make so free with someone else's kitchen.

Amy wished her host would return quickly, but then she recalled her state of dress. She might be fully covered but she felt half naked. Moreover, she realized, all her clothes were in that muddy pile in the corner. She no longer had any real clothes fit to wear.

She heard the back door slam and booted footsteps in the passageway.

# = 3 =

HARRY SHOOK OFF the cape and hung it up, grimacing at the muddy trail into the kitchen. Was it better to clean muddy floors when wet, or was one supposed to leave them to dry like clothes? He hoped the latter. Firkin had been given the day off, and with this weather he'd likely not bother to come back before tomorrow.

Harry sat on the bench and used the bootjack to pull off his wet boots, then put on his slippers.

He wondered who his unexpected guest was. She'd spoken like a lady but that worn-out old cart and the worn-out old horse in the shafts argued at the best genteel poverty.

He supposed she was a penny-pinched spinster of uncertain years and was now in a state of the vapors about being alone with a daring rogue. Well, he'd be charming to her and soon reassure her. He had a gift for charming females of all ages.

Reassuring smile in place, he walked into the kitchen.

And stopped dead.

Sitting beside the practical, mundane stove was an angel in a blanket, looking up at him with huge blue eyes.

Suddenly it registered. Frightened eyes.

Instinct took over. With scarce a moment's hesitation he said cheerfully, "Your nag's taken care of. I moved her into the stables, rubbed her down, and gave her a feed." He swung the kettle over the heat. "I'm sure you can use a cup of tea. I'm afraid I've not much food. Just bread and cheese and a Melton pie." He braced himself and looked at her. Still an angel, but a lot less frightened.

He risked a smile. "Would you like some?"

She smiled back. He could feel his heart begin to pound. He'd seen a lot of lovely women, but he'd never seen one as beautiful as this. Vague notions of fairies and bewitchment began to dance in his head, but he dismissed them. She was all too obviously flesh and blood, and here he was in a situation where it would be positively caddish to show how he felt.

It was an effort to keep the calm smile in place but he made it.

"I would like a piece of pie," she said softly. Her voice was as well bred as he'd thought and very musical.

He went and cut a slice of the pie. "Do you want to eat it there?" he asked.

The angel stood warily, holding on to the blanket. Harry watched, fascinated, unable to suppress the wicked hope that it might come loose and fall. But it stayed secure. With the cream wool down to the floor and the white towels over her shoulders the young woman looked like an Egyptian goddess except that Egyptian goddesses did not have clear blue eyes and an aureole of spun-gold curls.

She sat at the table and started in on the pork pie, her hunger confirming the fact that she was blessedly human. Harry made the tea, using the time to strengthen his self-control. When he was sure he could treat the vision like his Aunt Betty, he carried the pot to the table, along with two cups, a pitcher of milk, and the sugar bowl, then sat opposite. If all he could permit himself was a feast for the eyes, then at least he'd make the most of it.

"I must apologize for the state of the hospitality," he said lightly. "We only have one servant here and he's gone off to visit his sister. He was supposed to be back tonight, but with the weather he won't bother."

"We?" she asked, startled.

"It's all right," he reassured her. "They won't be back

either. They'll have racked up somewhere." He saw her relax and was pleased at how she trusted him. He just hoped he could prove worthy of that trust. "Coppice Farm belongs to my friend, Terance Cornwallis," he explained as she ate. "I'm staying here for the season with another friend, Charteris Ashby."

"Meltonians," she said with a trace of anxiety.

Harry could understand that. The avid hunters were little enough trouble when the scent was up and the hounds running, but if weather canceled the hunts, boredom often led to mischief.

"Not really," he said. "Meltonians are the great guns, the top of the trees. We've a way to go yet." Now that it had brewed, he poured tea into their cups. "I would like it if you would give me your name."

She was startled, which certainly did nothing to mute the effect of her eyes. She had clearly not thought that he did not know her. "Amy de Lacy," she said readily. "Of Stonycourt."

His first impression had been correct. She was a lady. A wild thought began to take possession of his mind. If he had to marry, why not marry an exquisite creature like this? Then he'd be entitled to look at her as much as he pleased and discover if the form beneath the blanket was as promising as it appeared.

He took a breath and stopped his imaginings before they appeared on his face. "I'm afraid I don't know the area very well," he said. "Is Stonycourt near here?"

She sipped from her cup of tea and gave what seemed to be an excessive sigh of pleasure. "About five miles away, over the Lincolnshire border."

"You're a long way from home."

Surprisingly, she colored. That did nothing for his control either. She looked like a naughty, tempting cherub. "I . . . I was supposed to be picking up some layers. We didn't expect such weather."

"No one did, or I doubt even my hunting-mad friends would have gone out."

She tilted her head to one side, and there was a glint

of teasing humor in her eyes as she said, "And are you not hunting mad?"

He laughed. "Caught, by Gad! Don't tell anyone."

"Certainly it's a heresy among men," she agreed.

"It's not that I don't like the sport," he assured her. "It's just that I'm not *mad* for it. There's nothing like a fine run on a clear crisp day, but to be slogging along on a soggy one is something I can do without."

Amy was feeling most peculiar. It was not just the rain and the cold followed by dry and warmth; it wasn't even the fact she was sitting here most unconventionally dressed, alone with a gentleman; it was the way he was behaving.

It wasn't that he was unaware of her looks—she'd seen a betraying flicker or two of astonishment. That didn't bother her, for without vanity her mirror told her every day that a person would have to be blind to not notice her beauty. But there was no heat in his eyes that made her want to hide, nor adoration to make her squirm. And he'd not said one word that could be construed as flirtatious.

It was like talking to Jasper.

It was wonderful.

She dared to tease again. "Did you read the comment of William Shenstone that the world may be divided into people that read, people that write, people that think, and fox hunters?"

He grinned. "He'd be strung up for that these days." He reached for the teapot and refilled their cups.

He was a handsome man, Amy thought, and handsomer when he laughed. She wasn't used to looking at men—she was more accustomed to avoiding them—but now she cautiously indulged a desire to study him.

He had light brown curly hair, hazel eyes, and a clean-cut face, but that wasn't the measure of his handsomeness. It was more the play of expressions on his face, particularly the teasing twinkle that could brighten his eyes and the way those eyes crinkled when he smiled. He was a man who was not afraid to smile.

She finished the last of her pie and tea and refused his offer of more. "When do you think I will be able to leave?" she asked.

"There's no way of telling," he said. "It's still throwing it down, and the roads will be in a terrible state even when it stops. I honestly don't think your horse would make it five yards in this, never mind five miles. I'll lend you one of ours if you want but we've only regular saddles. I'd come with you, of course, but it would still be a devil of a ride. Will your family be very worried?"

"I suppose they will," said Amy, "but it would be madness to go out just yet." She looked up anxiously. "But all the same, I can't spend the night here."

He smiled, and that warm smile allayed her anxiety like a potion. "For all that it's so dark out Miss de Lacy, that's just the storm. It's not quite three yet. There's plenty of time. If the worst comes to the worst, we'll walk over the hill to Ashridge Farm. The Coneybears will make you welcome, and your reputation will be safe there."

Amy frowned thoughtfully. "This obsession with night-time isn't very rational, is it? After all, there's nothing to stop us—" She caught her breath and stared at him. This wasn't Jasper.

"Not very rational, no," he said calmly, though she could see the twinkle in his eyes. "But as that's the way the world sees it, that's all we need to deal with."

"That's not quite the way the world sees it," she pointed out firmly. "There could be trouble just about me being here, especially dressed like this."

"But you look charmingly. You could set a new fashion."

Harry almost added that a beauty such as she could wear sackcloth and set a fashion but realized in time it would be a mistake. It really was incredibly difficult to treat this woman as if she were a sister. He didn't even have any sisters.

He pulled up a mental image of Chart's boisterous sister, Clytemnestra, and tried to think how he handled her. Just as if she were a boy. He realized his companion was speaking.

"It would have the advantage of economy," she agreed dryly. Then she frowned. "I have also to be concerned, however, about what I am to wear when I leave."

Harry was startled. He looked at the muddy pile which was her clothing. "And the only spare clothes in this house," he said "are men's."

"That would stir up the dust," she said. She was trying for a blasé tone but her anxiety showed through. "If I return home in any change of clothing, questions are sure to be asked. I do not wish to cause you any embarrassment."

Harry was considering that this might be the time to propose to her and soothe her fears, but his instinct told him it would not be a good idea.

She rose and went to inspect the muddy pile. "I think I'd better try to wash the dress."

"I can't imagine it will do any good."

She looked a reproach for such negative thinking. "What other choice do I have?"

Skeptically, Harry pulled out a tin tub and put it on the table. "I think this is what Firkin does the wash in if he does, but we have a woman in once a week for such things. What else do you need?"

"Water," Amy said. "Hot would be best, but I think we must make do with cold. There's no time to heat any if this is to be washed and dried. I need soap. I don't suppose you have any borax?"

"Not as far as I know." Harry passed over the bar of soap, then applied the pump and filled a bucket with water. As he poured it in the tub, Amy was paring fine strips off the soap into a dish full of the last hot water from the kettle.

Two buckets of water half filled the tub, and Amy poured in the liquid soap. Then she picked up the muddy lump which had been Beryl's blue stripe cambric and carried it at arm's length to the tub. Being careful not to splash herself, Amy sloshed the dress around and the water grew very muddy, very quickly.

"Good Lord," said Harry. "It's blue."

"Was," Amy said sadly. "It was my sister's favorite dress."

Harry was about to ask why she had been wearing it, especially on a mundane trip to pick up hens, but held his tongue. His original assumption of poverty was doubtless correct, and there could be all sorts of embarrassing reasons for the act.

He watched as she picked up the dress and banged it down, working out the dirt as best as she could. There was something strangely erotic about this delicate-looking beauty up to her elbows in suds. Perhaps it was seeing the silky roundness of her arms proving to be so capable.

She stood up with a sigh. "I think we'd better try fresh water."

Harry obediently tipped out the dirty water and filled the tub again. He'd never even considered the matter of laundry before, and here he was taking an active part. It was obvious that Amy de Lacy was familiar with the process. More evidence of abject poverty.

He imagined this poor family come down in the world and living in a cottage with only one good dress between them. It doubtless explained Miss de Lacy's self-possession while dressed so strangely. Perhaps, he thought—allowing his imagination full rein—they all wore blankets at home while waiting for their turn with the dress.

She was going to be overwhelmed when he asked her to marry him. He would provide all the comforts of life for her destitute family, and she would fall deeply in love with him.

"Do you have just the one sister?" he asked as she worried over the dress with the bar of soap, trying to get out some of the dirt around the hem.

"No, two," she answered readily. "Beryl's my older sister and Jacinth's my younger."

"Do you have any brothers?"

"Just one. Jasper."

He made the connection. "Beryl, Jasper, Jacinth, all

living at Stonycourt. Your parents must have been of a humorous disposition."

She looked up with a rueful smile. "Whimsical, at least."

"They should have called you Sapphire." It was out before he could stop it.

She looked slightly disappointed in him but merely said, "Or Aquamarine."

"How did you escape with Amy?"

"Simple good fortune," she said, once more bent to her work.

In the end she had to accept that she'd done all she could. The gown was now blue and the stripes could be seen, but there were heavy dirt stains fixed in the material, particularly around the hem. Amy hauled the garment out of the water and wrung it out as best she could, which wasn't very well. "I don't suppose you have a mangle," she said.

"I'm afraid not."

She looked around thoughtfully. "Do you mind the floor getting wetter?"

Harry looked down at the stone flags, which were awash with muddy water. "All the better to wash it with, I'd suppose."

She passed him the bodice of the dress and took the hem end herself. "Twist."

"Twist?"

He saw what she was doing and began to turn the cloth in the opposite direction, keeping it taut all the while. Water began to pour out.

"This can't be doing the garment much good," he pointed out.

"This garment is past its last prayers," said Amy twisting harder.

"Perhaps I should buy you a new one," he said.

"Why?" she asked with a blankly mystified look. "This is none of your doing."

Harry accepted it. He could hardly explain that he didn't want his future wife in rags, but he began to plan a wardrobe for her. He had never been much interested in women's clothes, but now he imagined Amy in cerulean blue silk with silver net; in dusky pink muslin trimmed with blond; in pristine white with roses in her hair.

He realized the work was getting harder as the dress became tight and began to twist on itself. Amy continued to turn her end, grimacing with the effort, determined to squeeze every last drop she could.

The dress coiled into a tighter and tighter bundle, and Harry and Amy were drawn closer and closer together. When Amy gave the final, grunting twist and said, "There!" she looked up and found herself inches from him.

Her mouth went dry and her head felt light. It was all that effort. She saw the fine chiseled shape of the end of his nose and thought it very pleasing indeed. She raised her eyes, and there was a warmth in his which shivered through her in the strangest way.

They were just standing there. She pulled the dress from his hold and hurried over to hang it in front of the stove, being careful that it couldn't catch fire.

That would be typical of today, she decided, that her clothes and her very shelter burn down around her ears.

As she stretched the cloth to try to lessen the creases she wondered what had made her feel so funny. It was this situation. In this predicament it was hardly surprising that she felt peculiar. For the first time in her life she would quite like to have a case of the vapors if she had any idea how to do it. She could at least appreciate the appeal. Just to let go, give up, and let someone else take care of everything.

Let him take care of everything?

She checked that her drapery was all securely in place and turned. He was looking out the window. He glanced at her. "Still very heavy," he said easily. "I think it will be at least an hour before it stops."

So he hadn't felt anything strange. That made her lapse even worse. Here was the one man she had met who treated her as a normal person and she was turning silly.

He was saying something else. "But you'll need that

long for your dress to even begin to dry. You know," he said as he left the window, "I don't feel it's at all wise for you to try to travel five miles in damp clothes on a chilly day."

"What else do you suggest?" Amy heard the edge of sarcasm in her voice and regretted it. She *was* dreading the trip home.

"You could go to Ashridge Farm, and I could ride over and reassure your family. Do you have parents still alive, by the way?" The question seemed to have importance for him.

"No, my father died two years ago, my mother six."

"I'm sorry. Who is your guardian, then?"

"My uncle, but he doesn't live with us. We have an aunt to lend us respectability." She couldn't understand why he seemed to find this displeasing, too. He must be a very high stickler. What would he think to find out that the de Lacys lived almost entirely in the kitchen—certainly in the winter months—and did almost everything for themselves because they felt guilty at asking anything of their two elderly and unpaid retainers?

"About Ashridge Farm," he prompted her.

Amy gathered her wits. "I suppose it is my only option," she admitted. "If you don't mind riding over to Stonycourt."

"I will be delighted," he said with a little bow.

He seemed to have turned rather serious. Amy felt uncomfortable with the lull in conversation and so she walked over to the table, hitching up her blanket so it didn't trail on the muddy floor. She studied the doll there. "It's an automaton!" she declared in delight.

He came to join her. "A broken one."

Amy sat down and touched the silk skirt with a gentle finger. "She's lovely. I had a doll once very like her. French, I think."

"Yes, but the mechanism is German. I'm mending her."

"Why?"

He looked up a little coolly. "Because otherwise she'd go on the rubbish dump."

Amy realized her question had seemed unfeeling and flushed. "I meant, why you?"

He sat down in front of the doll. "It's a hobby. I like to fix things, and these are often so beautiful it seems very worth the trouble. My mother finds them for me."

"You haven't told me anything of your family," she said. It was only a second later she knew that the curiosity she felt about this man was unwise.

"I'm an only child," he answered readily. "My mother and father are still living. Down in Hampshire."

"You're a gentleman," Amy said and tried to revive her teasing note. "You spend winter hunting, spring dancing and gambling."

"I don't gamble," he said with a lazy smile. "And I spend the summer sailing."

Amy's heart gave a little lurch. "Oh, I envy you!" Then she wished it unsaid. It was not wise to show one wanted things.

"You like to sail?" he asked. "Strange for a person living in the middle of the country."

"My father took us once with a friend," she said primly. "It was very pleasant." It was one of the best times of her life, but she didn't want him to know that.

He looked at her quizzically but then moved the automaton a little. "When I was interrupted," he said with a smile, "I was trying to see the state of the spring at the top of this lady's leg. I'll feel better about such a delicate operation now she has a chaperon."

Amy grinned at the thought. "Does my charge have a name?"

"Not as far as I know. Why don't you christen her?"

"Jane," Amy promptly said.

He looked at the elegant lady with the silk clothes and the high powered hairstyle. "She doesn't look like a Jane to me, but if you wish." He began to inch his fingers up the doll's leg.

Amy giggled and felt herself color. "As Jane's chaperon, I don't think I should allow you to do that, sir."

"Think of me as her doctor," he said, and something

in the way he said it set Amy's heart speeding. She was determined not to embarrass herself by showing it.

When he lifted the skirts to reveal layers of silk and lace petticoats, she protested again. "Really, sir! Can you not, as some doctors are supposed to do, examine by feeling alone?"

His eyes twinkled. "I'm afraid not." There was more to the words and the smile. Or Amy felt there was more. As his sensitive, long-fingered hands moved Jane's pale, porcelain leg Amy felt her face heat. She imagined his hands on her own leg.

He lifted that leg and stretched it.

Amy leapt to her feet.

He looked up and there was a flicker of humor in his eyes. "Is something the matter?"

"The dress," Amy gasped. "I must turn the dress!" She fled over to the hearth.

Parts of the gown were dry, but other parts were very damp. Amy rearranged the gown so that the thicker parts of the bodice and sleeves would be close to the heat, wishing she was near something cold, not hot, so she would have a chance to cool her burning face.

She couldn't think what had come over her. She had never had such thoughts before in her life. And with poor Mr. Crisp. The one man who had not ogled her, or protested his devotion, or done anything at all to embarrass her. And here she was having lewd thoughts about him.

When she'd finished with the dress, she sat in the chair by the fire but still watched him from half a room away.

He looked over. "Are you cold? There are more blankets."

"N—no." Amy swallowed. "I'd better keep an eye on the dress. It might scorch. I can preserve poor Jane's virtue from here."

He accepted it and they sat in silence as he worked, only the crackling of coal and the ticking of the kitchen clock to disturb the peace. His fingers were constantly entangled in the silk and lace of Jane's petticoats, and Amy's thoughts were extraordinary.

Then Amy realized the rain had stopped, and a glance

at the window confirmed this. There was even a lightening as the clouds lifted, but the natural darkness of evening was gathering.

She glanced at the clock. "It's five o'clock," she said. "I should go."

He looked up from his work. "So it is. We'll go in a minute, but I think I've fixed part of Lady Jane. It was just a loose connection. Come and look."

As if pulled by strings, Amy moved back to the table. He gave the key a few turns. A sweet, tinkling minuet started and the lady turned slightly. Her leg began to rise in an elegant and amazingly realistic manner.

There was a *ping*, and it collapsed limp again as the music slowed and stopped.

He laughed "A long way to go yet, I'm afraid."

Amy touched the silk skirt. "She will be lovely when she works, though."

"Yes."

She looked up and their eyes met. Amy knew there was something she wanted to say, but didn't know what it was.

His smile was rueful as he stood up. "You're right. It's time to go. I think it might be best if we don't tell the Coneybears you have been here at all. We can say you sheltered in the barn and only asked my help when the rain stopped."

"That sounds nonsensical to me," protested Amy.

His warm hazel eyes twinkled. "And you do not like to be thought foolish. Do you always do the sensible thing, Amy de Lacy?"

"I try," retorted Amy, for some reason feeling defensive. "You probably don't think that very womanly."

"Don't I?"

He was laughing at her. She quickly turned away. "I don't suppose so," she said. "You would doubtless approve of me far more if I had fainted out in the road and were sinking into the grave from inflammation of the lungs!"

"Now that makes *me* sound remarkably foolish."

He had come up behind her, and she could sense the warmth of his presence there. His hands settled over her towel-covered shoulders and turned her around.

Amy felt breathlessly dizzy as she looked up, and completely adrift. What was she doing? What was she supposed to be doing? What did she want to be doing?

He lowered his lips and touched them to hers. It was the lightest touch, velvet soft and warm. It was lovely.

Amy jerked her lips away but his hands prevented further escape.

"I'm sorry," he said gently. "I shouldn't have done that." He did did not sound repentant.

"No, no," she stammered. Then, "Yes. I mean you shouldn't have. We shouldn't have. . . ." His hands were still on her shoulders, a firm warm pressure which seemed to be seeping down into her as the damp chill had done so many hours ago.

"Perhaps not," he said, and his thumbs made little circles against her collarbone. "But it was not so terrible a sin." His right hand moved like a warm breeze across her shoulder to her bare neck. She gasped as she felt the soft brush of his fingers against her skin. She knew from his expression that he was thinking of more sinful things, and here she was, doing nothing to stop him.

He caught his breath and moved a yard or two away. "I do beg your pardon," he said. He looked around, as if at a loss, and his eyes fastened on her gown. "Perhaps your dress is dry."

Amy forced her limbs into movement and went to the dress. It was dry in parts but not in others but she had no intention of lingering here a moment longer. She knew what was happening here and it mustn't. It had only been a couple of hours. It was not too late. "It's dry enough," she said. "My family will be concerned. We must go to the farm quickly so that you can take a message to Stonycourt."

"Of course," he said, as if nothing significant had happened. But the power of the look in his eyes contradicted his tone and sent a shudder through her. "I'll just go upstairs and dress more warmly. You can put on your dress."

When he'd gone, the madness faded a little. Amy looked at her clothing in despair. For a supposedly sensible couple they'd not done very well. They'd done nothing about her shift, stockings, and shoes. What had they been thinking of?

# === 4 ===

AMY SPENT A few moments trying to gather the fortitude to put on her sodden, dirty shift but could not do it. Anyway, it was clearly nonsensical, and now above all times was the time to be sensible.

With a shudder she wriggled into the wet stockings. She could disguise the lack of a shift but she could hardly go barefoot and if she was to put on the soaking shoes she might as well bear the stockings. Then she put on the dress. At least it was warmly damp, not clammy.

When she came to fasten it she remembered the bottom button. Well there was nothing to be done about it.

He cleared his throat outside the door. "Is it all right for me to come in, Miss de Lacy?"

"Yes," she said.

He frowned when he saw her. "The sooner we get you to Ashridge and into dry clothes again, the better. Take the blanket to wrap around yourself."

Amy picked it up but said, "There is a button missing at the back of my gown. Do you have a pin to fasten it with?"

He came to look. It only then occurred to Amy that without her shift he would be looking at her bare back where the dress gaped. She didn't know why that seemed so dangerous, but it did.

"It doesn't matter," she said quickly.

"Hold on," he said, hands on her shoulders again, but impersonally. "I can fix it with my cravat pin."

Amy pulled herself out of his hold. "Don't be silly! That *would* set the cat among the pigeons."

He grinned. "I suppose it would. Never mind. It's only a small gap and it will be covered by the blanket. All set?"

As they walked down the passage toward the door, he said, "Look, there's an old pair of pattens here, belonged to Corny's aunt. Do you want to borrow them?"

"I think my shoes are past protection, but the pattens may keep me out of the mud." She tied them on and found the fit tolerable. The iron rings raised her a good three inches so that her eyes rose from his chin to his nose. She wasn't sure why this seemed significant.

She turned and *clink, clink, clinked* her way to the door.

"I don't know why you women insist on wearing those things," he said. "A pair of boots would be better."

Amy turned. "And needing a jack to get in and out of. Not very practical for a farm woman who's in and out all the time."

"And who has to clean the floors," he acknowledged. "I see what you mean."

He opened the door and they went out. The air was heavy with moisture and chill, too, but the wind had died down. Within her blanket, Amy was not too cold, though she knew her legs and feet would soon be frigid.

She was more concerned, however, with pondering this man's reaction to her contradiction. Experience had taught her that men did not like being told they'd said something silly, but she always forgot and told them anyway. This Mr. Crisp hadn't seemed to mind at all.

They crossed the muddy, bepuddled yard to a stile. Amy had to take his hand as she climbed over it, and the touch reminded her of that kiss. She looked at him, met his eyes, and looked away. This would not do at all.

They followed a footpath across a field of sheep and lambs, and Amy was glad of the pattens, which kept her feet above the soggy ground. The sheep watched the humans as they passed; the lambs gamboled forward and back, daring each other toward danger.

"Lambs are endearing, aren't they?" he said.

Amy thought so, too, but wanted no part of sweet sentiment today. "It's a shame they'll soon look as stupid as their mothers," she said flatly, "or end up as roast or stew."

He looked at her sharply. She met his eyes and saw his shock. That should nip any romantic nonsense in the bud.

But she was aware of a leaning toward sentiment herself, a desire to delight in lambs and courting birds, spring flowers and pretty ballads. She stamped on it firmly. She had to be ruthlessly practical.

It all came of having such an impractical family. How could she give in to nonsense when she had a brother who spent his book money on lottery tickets, sisters who believed that wishes would come true, and a father who had given no thought to the future.

Sir Digby had not been a desperate, haggard debtor; he'd been as happy as a bee in honey as long as he could somehow continue to provide fine wines, rich food, silk dresses, and prime horses for his family.

Amy couldn't understand such a mentality at all.

"Don't look so worried," her companion said. "It'll take me no time at all to ride over to your place and reassure your family."

She realized they must have been walking for some time. They were coming to the end of the sheep pasture; Coppice Farm was behind some trees, and another, more prosperous farm was ahead at the top of the rise. Presumably Ashridge.

"I'm sorry. I was woolgathering."

He smiled. "Very appropriate among a field of sheep, and these seem to have a fine thick fleece."

They came to a gate. As he opened it he picked a long tuft of wool from the hedge. After they were through and the gate was securely shut, he gave it to her with a smile. "A fleece for your thoughts?"

She took it and rubbed it between her fingers, feeling the grease in it. "Just family troubles, Mr. Crisp." She determined to make sure he had no illusions. "You'll doubtless have realized we don't have much money."

"I don't think any the less of you for it."

"So I should think," Amy retorted. "Money isn't the sole determinator of quality, Mr. Crisp."

He raised his brows. "Has anyone ever told you you've got a damned sharp edge to your tongue, Miss de Lacy?"

He was daring to criticize her. "Yes," she said. "Doubtless the same people who tell you you've got an uncouth edge to yours."

"Uncouth!" He caught his breath and his temper. "All I meant, Miss de Lacy, was that I don't look down on you or your family for being poor, as I'm sure other people do, it being the way of the world. Is that deserving of rebuke?"

"I—" Amy caught herself, too. What was going on? She was normally the most moderate of people. "I am sorry," she said sincerely. "And after you've been so kind. I'm just not myself, Mr. Crisp, and you're right, there are family problems, but not ones I can discuss with a stranger. Please excuse my outburst."

They had come to a stop during their spat, and now he touched her elbow to urge her on toward the gate which led into the yard of Ashridge Farm. "You are excused. This must have been an ordeal." He stopped by the gate and smiled at her in a way that reminded her of that strange time in the warm kitchen. "I don't suppose you could bring yourself to call me Harry, by way of reparation."

Amy felt a pang of alarm. "Of course not," she said, rather more sharply than she had intended.

"No, of course not," he repeated without offense as he ushered her through the gate. "But despite our brief acquaintance I feel very at ease with you, almost like a brother. I have no sisters, though, so I don't know how a brother really feels."

Relieved at his light tone, Amy grinned at him. "Blue-deviled, I think. Jasper seems to think his sisters are his cross to bear."

He smiled. "My friend Chart appears to feel the same way, but protective, too. Toward his younger one at least."

"Poor Jasper has only older sisters. Even his twin came into the world ahead of him."

They crossed another muddy yard, and the farmhouse door opened before they got there. In it stood a pretty, brown-haired, brown-eyed girl in cap and apron. "Good day to you, Mr. Crisp."

"Good day, Meg. This lady got caught in the rain near our place. I was hoping your mother would give her shelter for the night. Then I can ride over and tell her family she's safe."

The girl was already standing back and urging them in.

In moments, Amy was in a proper kitchen. Pots were bubbling on the hob, filling the place with warm, aromatic steam. Five loaves sat cooling, adding their own perfume. A big pie sat on a table already laid for dinner.

Mrs. Coneybear came forward. "Oh, the poor young lady! Come stir the gravy, Meg, while I see to things. Why," the gaunt woman said as she came toward them, "it's Miss de Lacy, isn't it?"

"Miss Amy de Lacy," Amy said. "I'm surprised to be recognized so far from home."

The women chuckled. "Once seen, never forgotten, dear. Saw you at Stamford market last year. Are you wet? Oh dear, you are. You'll catch your death. Now, Mr. Crisp, if you're to ride over to Stonycourt, you'd best be on your way. Night's coming."

And so Amy found her good samaritan gone without a special farewell, but she scarce had time to consider if this was a good thing or not as she was sent off with a talkative Meg to find dry clothes.

"Put us all in a tizzy, I'll tell you, having three fine young gentlemen a-come and live next door. Very nice, they be, when all's said and done. They come over now and then to get milk and eggs and such, seeing as they mostly have just the one servant."

She opened a wardrobe within which the clothes hung on hooks and pulled out a green print gown. "Here, try this, miss. It'll doubtless be a mite tight around the top, but it's this or nothing, for Ma's flat as a board, despite having bore five kiddies."

She cheerfully helped Amy out of her gown and didn't say anything about the lack of a shift but produced one of her own. Amy wondered what she was thinking, and could feel her face heat up. She wanted to protest her innocence but knew that would be the worst thing to do.

"Yes," Meg went on, "Ma said it was as well I was already smitten with Martin Howgarth before those three turned up, or I might have gone and done something silly."

Was that a sly dig?

"Course, that Mr. Ashby's the handsomest. But he's got a bit too much of an air to him for my taste. Grandson of a duke, he is, so they say. And Mr. Cornwallis, he's a lovely man, but ever so shy. He stays here most of the year, so we see a lot of him. Ma has him over for dinner every now and then. She seems to think he'll starve to death, though you only have to look at him to see that b'ain't likely to be his problem."

Amy was in the dress and Meg was forcing the buttons together. "I'm not sure it will fit," Amy protested.

"Course it will," Meg said cheerfully, and gave another tug, which rendered Amy nearly as flat as Mrs. Coneybear. "Which do you think's the most handsome?" Meg asked.

Amy found once the buttons were fastened, it was not too uncomfortable. In a small mirror, she could see the effect was rather like a Tudor stomacher. Her bosom was flattened out. She was thinking of adopting the style when she remembered she was supposed to be flaunting her assets, not concealing them.

"Well?" Meg prompted.

Amy remembered the question. "I . . . er . . . only saw Mr. Crisp. I'm not sure any other gentlemen were at home."

"Out hunting," said Meg, with a nod of her head as she gathered up the dress and stockings. "Mad for it, they be. I'll put these in to soak, will I?"

"Do you think it will do any good?" Amy asked.

"Can't hurt," said Meg, heading for the door. "Come you down. The men'll be in for dinner in a moment. I think Mr. Crisp is nicest. And he's good enough looking when he smiles. He's got a lovely smile."

"Yes," said Amy wistfully. "I suppose they're all very rich," she said, not really believing it.

"They're not short a groat," said Meg with a flashing grin over her shoulder. "Mr. Ashby paid a hundred guineas for a horse a few weeks back. A hundred guineas! Da couldn't get over it. But I don't reckon they're rich by your standards. Mr. Crisp and Mr. Ashby are oldest sons, though, so they'll come into a fair bit one day I suppose."

Not soon enough to be any use to me, thought Amy.

Meg dumped the dress and stockings in a tub and disappeared. In a few moments she was back with a large bucket of hot water. She pumped in some cold, then added hot, then threw in some softened soap and some liquids.

"What are they?" Amy asked.

"Turpentine and hartshorn. Works a treat on stuff like this."

Full of energy, Meg grasped a dolly-stick and started to pummel the garments with it. Amy felt exhausted just watching her.

"They'll never be the same, but they might be wearable," Meg said cheerfully. She considered Amy as she worked. "You're a grand looker, miss. Mr. Crisp was giving you the eye." She gave a cheeky wink. "You interested in him?"

"No," said Amy quickly.

Meg accepted it. "I suppose most men make a sheep's eye at you," she said without a trace of envy. "He's going to be a lord, though, one day. You could do worse."

"He is?" He'd avoided giving her that information. Amy wondered why.

Meg nodded. "Can't remember lord of what. There!" She hauled out the dolly and hung it on the wall. "We'll just let them soak." There was a shout from the kitchen.

"Come on, Ma'll need my help, and you look as if you could do with some food."

Amy trailed slowly after. She realized her day's misadventures had exhausted her, but she wondered if she had ever had the bursting vitality of Meg Coneybear. Perhaps it was as well fate had destined her to be ornamental rather than useful.

She shook off that depressing thought and told herself it was simple lack of food that made her so mawkish.

If that was the problem, she had come to the right place to solve it. Even in their prosperous days, the de Lacys had not eaten with the gusto of the Coneybears. She could quite see that the thought of the young men living on bread and cheese would wound Mrs. Coneybear to the heart.

Ten people sat to the table, including Amy. There were Mr. and Mrs. Coneybear, Meg, three robust sons, two working men, and a healthy young giant who turned out to be Martin Howgarth, Meg's intended. Amy understood why Meg had not had her head turned by the young gentlemen at Coppice Farm, for Martin was handsome enough and plainly adored the girl.

His warm attention to his bride-to-be had a strange effect on Amy. She wished she was loved like that. She wished she had some chance of being loved like that. A mercenary marriage seemed unlikely to produce that kind of devotion.

The huge pie was steak and kidney, and it was served with masses of potatoes, turnips, and greens and great slabs of bread and butter. It was followed by a choice of damson pie or bilberry, both with custard. The men consumed vast quantities, washing it down with homebrewed ale. When they'd finished, they sat nibbling at cheese, just to keep starvation at bay.

Amy had seen all the men's eyes widen at first looking at her, but they'd been too concerned with the food to make anything of it. Now, however, as Meg and her mother cleared the table and the pipes came out, Amy saw a selection of looks directed at her. Mostly they were just frankly admiring, though Amy feared the youngest Coneybear son had a touch of idolatry in his eyes. And one of the farm workers had a lustful gleam in his eye.

She decided it was time to disappear. She rose to her feet. "Thank you for the meal, Mrs. Coneybear. It was delicious. I'm afraid, after my adventure, I feel very tired. Could you show me where I could sleep?"

The lustful man sniggered, but a stern look from Mrs. Coneybear shut him up.

"Course, dear," the woman said. "You can sleep with Meg. Just you go up. Meg'll come up in a minute with a hot brick."

"Oh, that's's not necessary."

"We don't want you taking pneumonia, Miss de Lacy. You do as I tell you. You'll feel more the thing in the morning."

Amy was no sooner in the bedroom than Meg scampered in after her, pulled out a flannelette nightgown, and gave it her. Then she was gone.

Amy changed and slipped into the bed, which was not very cold. Within minutes Meg was back with the brick wrapped in layers of flannel. She pushed it in by Amy's feet. "One thing," she said cheerfully, "you'll have the bed right cozy for me by the time I come up."

At the door she turned. "What d'you think of him, then?"

For a second, Amy assumed she meant Harry Crisp, but then she realized her mistake. "Mr. Howgarth seems a pleasant man, and very handsome."

Meg's face lit up in a starry smile. "Isn't he? We're to be married come June. I can hardly wait."

Her meaning was earthy and direct and wholesome.

After she'd gone, Amy lay thinking of that amiable giant: of his warm lazy smile following his darling as she bustled about the room, of his solidly muscled forearms and his hairy chest showing at the vee of his open shirt.

The thoughts slid over, somehow, to Harry Crisp. She had seen no part of his body except his hands and face.

Would she see him again? Or would she be returned home by the Coneybears?

She shouldn't see him again. She was a fortune hunter, and he didn't have the kind of fortune she required. And he seemed able to stir in her wanton thoughts the like of which she had never experienced before; thoughts which made her want to consign Owen Staverley and all other wealthy bachelors to the devil.

She wiped away a slow trickle of tears. They were just tiredness. That was all they were. Amy fell asleep before Meg joined her and woke after the girl had gone. That was hardly surprising, for she could tell by the sun that it must be the middle of the morning. Feeling like a slugabed, she leapt out of bed and washed her face and hands in the water provided. She felt a great deal more like herself and able to face anything.

She remembered her weak, sentimental feelings of the night before and laughed, dismissing them as the product of an overly tired mind.

To her amazement, Beryl's dress was laid on a chair, faded but with nearly all the stains removed, and pressed almost to elegance. Her poor mistreated stockings were snowy white and, she saw when she picked them up, neatly darned in two places where there had been no darn before.

She detected Meg's indefatigable work and sighed. She felt such a useless, ornamental creature next to the robust girl. It was both reassuring and disconcerting to remember that Martin Howgarth had not given the beautiful Amy de Lacy a moment's more attention than he'd had to, but had cared only for his bride-to-be. Clearly a man who knew a treasure when he found one.

Had they walked out together last night, Meg and Martin, holding hands in the moonlight, talking of plans for their home and their family? Perhaps stopping for a kiss.

Amy walked down the stairs to the busy kitchen. She could hear Meg and her mother chattering away accompanied by the clatter of constant work. The chatter was mostly Meg's. Amy smiled, realizing that even after such a brief acquaintance, she would miss the girl.

She walked into the kitchen and stopped dead. Three young men were tucking into huge plates of sausage, eggs, and fried bread.

The one facing her, a rotund young man with gingerish hair, froze, a forkful of food midway to his mouth.

Alerted, the other two swiveled.

Harry Crisp rose to his feet, his charming smile lighting his face. "Miss de Lacy. You are looking a great deal better."

Amy gave him her hand and a smile and turned to his companion. The second man grinned at her appreciatively as he slowly rose to his feet. He was as tall and broad as Harry Crisp, but dark haired and gray eyed. He was an altogether handsomer and bolder specimen. His fine eyes gleamed with appreciation, yet Amy could not take offense. It was the unabashed acknowledgment of one fine bird for another.

Harry followed her eyes. "Allow me to present my friends, Miss de Lacy. Chart Ashby and Terance Cornwallis."

By this time the rotund one had come to his senses. He dropped his fork and got to his feet to stammer an incoherent greeting.

Chart Ashby took her hand and kissed it with lingering expertise. Amy just gave him a humorous look; she knew the type. It was Harry Crisp who took offense, drew her away, and guided her to a seat at the table. The gentlemen all sat down. Meg bustled over with a plate full of food and a mug of tea, which she placed before Amy with a cheerful smile.

Amy wondered how she could eat a fraction of it, but clearly the men would not feel happy about eating until she was, so she started.

When she'd swallowed the first mouthful she turned to Harry Crisp. "Were my family worried?"

He frowned slightly. "Not really. I suppose they know you're a sensible person who would seek shelter." He looked up at her gave a slight wink, which reminded her that they shared secrets.

Amy colored and broke eye contact. This caused her gaze to fall on the handsome Mr. Ashby, who was looking intrigued. She felt her face heat even more. He had the look of a man who noticed things and would not be above making mischief if it suited him.

"They certainly know I'm sensible," she said firmly and cut another piece of sausage. "I'm famous for it. I hope they made you welcome." She considered the delicious sausage and remembered that yesterday's dinner was to have been potato pie. Looking down at the feast on her plate, she wondered what he'd made of it.

"I came straight back," he said, "in case you needed reassurance. But you were already in bed. Mrs. Coneybear gave me some leftovers."

"Mrs. Coneybear's leftovers would delight the Regent himself," said Chart Ashby, directing a brilliant smile at the farmer's wife.

There was a touch of red in the woman's cheeks as she grinned. "Go on with you, Mr. Ashby."

He turned the same smile on Amy. "Fortunate for us you were so far from home, Miss de Lacy."

Amy stiffened. She found his manner altogether too warm. "What do you mean by that, sir?"

His smile broadened. "Why, only that you have given us an excuse to come begging at Mrs. Coneybear's table."

Amy felt tricked into the wrong. Thank heavens this man had not been alone at Coppice Farm yesterday. Heaven knows what would have become of her. She saw a look flash between Harry Crisp and his friend, and with a smile Mr. Ashby returned his attention to his food.

Harry said, "I believe your aunt was concerned. It appears you hadn't made it clear where you were going. But your sister was sure you would be safe, but for some reason she seemed to think you would be at Prior's Grange at Upper Kennet."

Amy could feel guilt rise in her cheeks. "I wonder why," she said lightly, then lied shamelessly. "I'm afraid

Beryl thinks she has powers of precognition. She likes to guess things, but she's rarely correct."

Chart Ashby laid down his knife and fork. "If she guessed Upper Kennet with nothing to go on she got remarkably close. Perhaps you should charge for her services."

"A miss is as good as a mile, as they say," Amy retorted and addressed herself to Harry. "I must thank you again for riding over, sir. And now, will Zephyr be fit for the return journey?"

All three young men appeared to have a choking fit at the name. Amy struggled but then she burst out laughing. "It is ridiculous," she admitted as she wiped away tears. "But she was probably young and speedy once."

"Not with those hocks," said Mr. Cornwallis seriously.

Amy looked at him. "Oh dear, and I'd always consoled myself with the thought of her flighty youth."

Mr. Cornwallis colored and stuffed more fried bread in his mouth.

"Whatever her past," said Harry, "she appears as able as she was yesterday, and I've mended the ribbons. I think you can make it home, but of course we'll escort you to make sure."

"Oh, that's not at all necessary," Amy said. She needed to put the full five miles between herself and Harry Crisp as soon as possible.

"It assuredly is, " he said. "Besides, Corny's fellow, Firkin, did try to get back yesterday and slipped and twisted his leg. He's laid up at his sister's for the next few weeks. We thought we'd ride over to a friend of ours after seeing you safe, see if he can put us up for a day or two while we find a replacement." He winked up at Mrs. Coneybear. "We did ask if we could hire Meg, but her mother won't have it."

Mrs. Coneybear gave a wry smile. "Quite apart from the fact that I need her here, Mr. Crisp, as they say around here, 'tis a foolish shepherd what puts sheep in with wolves."

Meg giggled and flashed a look at Chart Ashby. He

made a gesture of mock alarm. "Don't flirt with me, girl. Martin'll tear my arms off!"

"That he will," Meg said saucily and went off on an errand with a laugh and a swing of her hips.

Her mother sighed. "I'll be glad to see that one safely wed. So you'll be away a few days, sirs. I'm sorry to hear about Josh Firkin, but I'm sure I can find you someone if you want me to look."

As they discussed this, Amy messed aimlessly with the remains of the food on her plate, until she realized what she was doing and stopped it. Why did she envy Meg so?

Because Meg was so sure of her place in her family's affections, and in those of her husband-to-be. And doubtless in the Howgarth family, wherever they were.

These days Amy's family seemed to see her only as a taskmaster and a wet blanket, and Jassy, at least, envied her beauty. The future offered little chance of improvement. Either she must continue to bully her family into economy or sell herself to the highest bidder. She could hardly expect a man who bought beauty to have the kind of wholesome warmth Martin showed for Meg. And if she married an older man for his money, his family would surely all hate her.

A hand covered hers. She looked up. It was Harry Crisp. They were alone. She could hear Mrs. Coneybear talking to the other men outside.

"What is it?" he asked seriously. "Do you not feel well?"

Amy pulled her hand away. "I feel perfectly well. Are we ready to go?"

She would have left the kitchen, but he detained her with a gentle hand on her arm. "You are unhappy, Miss de Lacy. I wish you would tell me why. Is it your family?"

Amy had the strangest urge to lean against his broad chest and have all her problems soothed away.

He spoke again. "I couldn't help but think your family were not as concerned as I would expect, Miss de Lacy."

"Don't criticize them," she said sharply, stepping away. "It is as you said. They knew I could take care of myself."

He stiffened and removed his hand. "I'm sure you can, too," he said coolly, "but I would still be concerned if you were out in a storm."

Despite the coolness, there was a message in his eyes which a part of Amy hungered to read but another part knew would be disastrous. "You have been very kind, sir," she said flatly, "but my safety, and my high or low spirits, are none of your concern."

With that she finally made her escape.

$$== 5 ==$$

TRUE TO THEIR WORD, the three young men escorted her home, but Zephyr's ambling pace was too much for their patience, and they took turns at racing off across nearby fields and setting their mounts at a variety of obstacles, often at hair-raising speed.

Amy couldn't help thrilling at their magnificent horsemanship, even as she told herself they were reckless fools and that Mr. Owen Staverley would prove to be a quiet, restful companion in life.

Harry Crisp chose to escape rather less often than the others, and showed less impatience with ambling alongside the cart chatting to Amy.

"You're going to have to retire poor Zephyr soon," he said at one point.

"I know," said Amy with a sigh. "But that will leave us entirely without transportation." She was perfectly happy to hammer home their destitution in order to squelch any inconvenient tendencies on his part.

"You could replace her for a few guineas," he pointed out. "Surely that would be a good investment."

"A few guineas may seem nothing to you, sir, but we simply do not have it to spare."

She saw him raise his brows skeptically, but he did not persist. "Then I suppose you will have to depend on neighbors for assistance. When you need to go into Stamford or such like."

"I am sure they will be pleased to help if it should

become necessary," Amy said, hearing the chill in her voice. It was perhaps ungracious, but she felt as if she were being interrogated. The fact was that their friends and neighbors had been very kind, but the de Lacys had refused most offers of help. They could not be forever accepting hospitality they could not return.

"Miss de Lacy," he said with a frown, though not unkindly. "I fear you are ill advised. It can happen to anyone, to fall on hard times, and I am sure your friends and neighbors would take pleasure in helping you until your family has restored itself."

She looked up at him in irritation. "You make it sound," she sharply, "like a frosted plant which will grow lush with time and sunshine, sir. In fact, the family is a group of people who are teetering on a razor's edge between destitution and a chance of a prosperous future. Only hard work and constant vigilance will prevent disaster."

"I think you worry too much," he said blandly, making her want to hit him. "But if so, all the more reason to let your friends and neighbors help you."

"Your mount is looking restive, Mr. Crisp," she said pointedly. "Would he not enjoy a gallop?"

He looked thoughtfully at her, not obviously dismayed by the dismissal. "It does all creatures good to run free," he said and turned the big bay toward the fields. He entered decorously enough through a gate but then set an alarming pace toward a fence and flew over it, then headed for the next.

In this low-rising countryside, it was easy to watch his progress over hedge and fence and gate. He was a fine rider—courageous but also considerate of his horse.

Amy sighed, wishing she were riding with him. If she still had Cloud, her favorite mount, she could offer a fair challenge. She had usually held her own against Jasper, and the four years' difference in age surely didn't matter in such things, as his best horse, Caligula, had been a hand taller than Cloud.

They seemed so long ago, those carefree times. Riding

parties, dancing, picnics. The hunt had met at Stonycourt once a season, the mounted host taking a stirrup cup before setting off. The de Lacy men had always been among the best mounted.

They could regain it all, she told herself firmly, with prudence and management. The hunt would meet again at Stonycourt, with Jasper as the host. There would be dowries and a Season for Jassy, at least. All it needed was management and a rich marriage.

Harry Crisp headed back, flat out, aiming to leap the high bushy hedge onto the road behind her. She gasped and twisted to watch.

The bay gathered and soared over the brush without fault. But a plover was flushed and flapped up noisily from beneath the horse. The horse landed awkwardly, almost going down. Heart in mouth, Amy saw the skill and strength used to hold him and right him.

Harry leapt off and went to the jibbing, trembling horse's head to quiet him.

Amy pulled up Zephyr and ran over. "Is he all right?" The damned man could kill himself with that sort of insanity!

"Yes. Just bothered a bit. There, boy," he said, rubbing the bay's nose. "It's my fault not yours." He looked ruefully at Amy. "I should know to be cautious with that kind of thick hedge."

She nodded sternly. "Yes, you should. I don't know what you were about."

He smiled lazily. "I was trying to impress you, of course."

Amy stared helplessly at him, then, face rosy, she hurried back to the dogcart. The way her heart had leapt at his words was positively terrifying.

For the remainder of the journey, Harry Crisp rode decorously alongside the cart but in silence. Amy was aware of him, however, all the time, whereas Chart Ashby and Terance Cornwallis could have ridden off the edge of the world without her being any the wiser.

When they turned in the gates of Stonycourt, all three

men settled to riding nearby, looking and admiring the rolling meadows and occasional stands of trees. There had been a great many more trees once, but they had been felled, some by her father to provide money for extravagances but most since his death to feed the gaping maw of their debts. They would all have gone except that Jasper had put his foot down and declared he refused to have his land completely deforested.

Nothing Amy had said had moved him.

Now Amy admitted Jasper might have had a point. To a person who had never seen it in better days, Stonycourt Park looked well enough today.

"I am perfectly safe now, gentlemen," she said as the house came in sight. "I thank you for your escort."

"Not at all," said Chart Ashby. "Take you to your door, Miss de Lacy. This is a very pleasant property."

In the spring sun the house and grounds did look almost as they had. It brought tears pricking at Amy's eyes but it was also undoing all her good work in deterring Harry Crisp.

"Burdened with debts," said Amy bluntly.

"But full of potential," said Chart, looking around with a shrewd eye. "Fine land."

Amy cast a quick glance at Harry Crisp to see if he was as impressed as his friend. His face was unreadable. "All leased," she countered, "and the income being used to pay interest and reduce debt."

"What? All of it?" asked Chart, startled.

"Yes," replied Amy firmly.

They had come in sight of the house. Amy loved Stonycourt, but at this moment she could have wished it a moldering ruin. Instead it rested in placid beauty in its landscape, as handsome as ever. It was a substantial, plain three-story stone building with a two-story wing at each side. There was no ornament to it at all—not even a portico over the door. It owed its beauty to perfect proportions and simplicity. It would take a long time for poverty to take those away, and the fact that there now were sheep grazing right up to the drawing-room windows meant that they had a well-groomed sward in all directions.

"Why?"

Startled out of her thoughts, Amy realized it was Harry Crisp who had spoken. "Why what?" she asked.

"Why does all the income go to service the debt?"

"Is that any of your business, sir?"

He raised a brow. "I suppose not, but you seem determined to air your family's woes, and I am curious."

Amy could feel her cheeks heat. "It was not my intention to burden you with my family problems. I merely find it detestable to be pretending to be something other than the truth. As for our financial arrangements, we do not starve and my brother attends school, but we prefer to live simply for a few years to set the estate on a sound footing once more."

"Very frugal," he said without obvious approval, "but I think the estate could bear the burden of a few indulgences. Another nag, for example. I'll act as your agent to buy one if you want." When she did not immediately agree, he said with an edge, "I engage to pay less than the cost of that dress you ruined yesterday."

Amy could think of nothing to say. He thought her the sort of feather-headed fool who would fret about a guinea or two while carelessly ruining a valuable garment, and there was no explanation she could make. She was relieved that they had arrived at the house at last.

Beryl appeared, flushed with excitement, trailed by the ever-watchful Prettys. Amy made the introductions but managed to forestall Beryl's attempts to invite them in.

Then Aunt Lizzie appeared to support Beryl, but Amy grimly prevailed and soon the men were mounted again.

But then Chart Ashby said, "Hume House is only a couple of miles cross-country from here, Miss de Lacy. Can I hope we'll be welcome if we call to see how you are?"

What could she possibly say but yes?

\* \* \*

"Three handsome heroes!" declared Beryl ecstatically as soon as the door was closed. "Amy, dearest, you've outdone yourself. One for each of us!"

"But why you didn't want to invite them in, Amethyst," said Aunt Lizzie, "I cannot imagine. Very rag-mannered."

"What on earth could we have offered them?" Amy demanded. "I doubt they have a taste for chamomile tea."

"I doubt I have either," sniffed Lizzie. "I don't know why you won't let us buy just a little bohea to add to it. Anyway, I do believe there is a quarter bottle of brandy left. That would be more to their taste."

"After our grand lottery party," said Amy, "that is all we have. We had better preserve it carefully, not waste it."

"It wouldn't be wasted," Lizzie pointed out. "It would be more in the way of an investment. You have to make men comfortable if you wish to attract their interest, Amethyst."

"I have no desire to attract their interest," said Amy firmly.

Beryl laughed her disbelief. "But they are handsome and charming and all you could desire!"

Amy said, "Except rich."

This was drowned by Aunt Lizzie's, "Shame about London, though. They say Tsar Alexander's going to be visiting in June."

Amy could feel a familiar exasperation creeping up her neck to form a headache.

Pretty, who was hovering—in case there was something to be learned rather than making himself useful—muttered, "I thought you was off after that Staverley gent, Miss Amy."

"So I was, Pretty," said Amy crisply. "For heaven's sake, Beryl, those poor young men just assisted me. Are you going to shackle them for it?" When she saw the hurt disappointment on her sister's face she was immediately contrite. "I'm sorry, love. Indeed, Mr. Ashby did say he might ride over to call. Perhaps you can engage his interest."

Beryl brightened a little. "Is he the dark one? Oh no.

I'm sure he's too much of a high-flier for me. What about the portly one with the friendly smile?"

Amy was going to protest her sister's self-denigration, but had to acknowledge that it was true. It was impossible to imagine the arrogant, though charming, Chart Ashby and her plain, sweet-natured sister having anything in common. "Mr. Cornwallis," she supplied. "He's very shy, so I haven't shared more than a couple of words with him, but he does seem very pleasant." There was no harm in encouraging Beryl's dreams a little, and heaven knows, if she could find herself a husband, that would be one less person depending on Amy for survival.

Beryl linked her arm happily with Amy's and led her toward the kitchen. "So that leaves the two dashing ones for you and Jassy."

"Jassy's far too young!" Amy protested. "Where is she anyway?"

"She's walked over to the Burford's to visit Amabelle. Tell me all your adventures."

Amy wasn't up to objecting to Jassy's outing, though she would return discontented and with a charity package from Amabelle Burford's mama. She decided to give Beryl and Aunt Lizzie the official version of her adventure and mention nothing of the hours spent in a blanket in Harry Crisp's kitchen.

Aunt Lizzie frowned as she made the herb tea, both at the concoction and the story. "Why did you linger in the barn in your wet clothes, you silly girl? You could have caught your death!"

"But I would have had to cross the yard to get to the house, and it was raining so hard," Amy pointed out. "And it was a good thing I stayed where I was, for Mr. Crisp was all alone in the house. That would never have done."

Aunt Lizzie got a calculating look in her eyes. "Seems to me it would have done very well indeed, dear. He'd have been smitten . . . likely have become a bit carried away . . . honorable thing and all that."

Amy felt sick at the thought and took a deep breath to

stop herself saying something unforgivable. "That would have been disastrous, Aunt," she pointed out. "He's not rich enough."

Lizzie splashed boiling water on the leaves. "Ugh. I don't care what you say, this might be good medicine but it isn't *tea*. You can carry this fortune-hunting thing too far, Amethyst" she said. "A bird in the hand, and all that. He's doubtless warm enough to keep you in comfort and to help your sisters along a bit. Don't be greedy."

Amy sat down at the table, feeling as if she'd stepped back into a quagmire after a few brief hours of relief. "Even if that were so," she said, "how could we all marry and go away, leaving Jasper here at a Stonycourt crippled with debts? And the Prettys must have their pension," she continued, "and you, Aunt, should have enough to live in comfort in London near your friends."

"That would be nice," admitted Lizzie. "You're a kind, thoughtful girl really, Amethyst." She brought over the tea, and the three women sat down at the table. "Are you sure they're not rich?" she asked.

Amy realized she didn't know for sure, but she wanted to squelch these notions. "Not particularly," she answered firmly. "They all will have to wait years before they are in control of their fortunes. They aren't in a position to pour money into the estate or provide dowries."

"You mustn't worry about us, dearest," said Beryl. "Truly, I am quite resigned to being a maiden aunt. I will dote on your children. I will look after Jasper until he finds a bride and then go where I can be most useful."

She was being completely honest, thought Amy, which made it even worse. Beryl the dreamer had bravely scaled her dream down to fit her circumstances. Amy was determined she should have more. "Beryl, that is all nonsense," she said briskly. "I have no particular interest in any of my rescuers, or they in me. In fact, in Mr. Crisp's case, it was refreshing to encounter one male who did not lose his wits over me. That dratted storm ruined my plan to meet Mr. Staverley, but I will think of another." She looked ruefully at the dress. "I am sorry about this, Beryl."

Beryl drained her cup and got to her feet. "All in a good cause," she said. "It's time you stopped wearing your usual dismal clothes anyway. Let's have it off you and see what can be done. It has at least held its shape."

Amy followed her sister upstairs. "I'm afraid it's beyond repair, dear."

Beryl looked at the dress again. "We'll see. I think I'll dye it a darker shade and put a flounce around the hem to hide the stains. You'll be surprised."

In her room Amy stripped off the hard-used garment and passed it over. She wouldn't be surprised if Beryl managed to revive it. She was very good at that sort of thing. She saw Beryl looking at her shift in surprise. "That isn't yours."

"No," said Amy praying that she wouldn't blush. "It belongs to the daughter of the farm where I stayed the night. Mine was completely ruined."

"I don't see how it could be more ruined than the dress," Beryl said with mild disapproval. "I'm sure I could have mended it. Really, Amy," she said as she left, "sometimes you just aren't very practical."

Amy collapsed on the bed in giggles.

Eventually she sobered. She'd left her shift in Harry Crisp's house, and it was monogrammed. Beryl insisted on embroidering their initials on all their personal garments. What would happen if it were found?

Piers Verderan, Lord Templemore, was in the stables of Hume House when Harry, Chart, and Corny rode in. He was studying the gait of a fine gray thoroughbred which was being led around by a groom. Verderan, as he still preferred to be called, was a handsome, elegant man with crisp, dark curls, which gave him a distinctly devilish look and contributed to his nickname of the Dark Angel.

He looked at the trio with a sigh, but there was a smile in his deep blue eyes. "Can't be the faulty roof this time," he said.

"Faulty servant," said Chart blithely as he swung off

his horse. "Broken leg. If it ain't convenient, Ver, it don't matter. Melton will be pretty empty this time of year."

Verderan smiled, an open smile which would have startled his acquaintance a year ago. "But life's been so dull these last weeks," he said. "Renfrew was our sole hope of enlivenment, but he's buried in his plans for this place. Once we remove, he's to take it all in hand." He turned to the groom holding the gray. "He looks fit, Pritchett. Put him in the paddock."

Another groom came forward to take the guests' mounts, and the gentlemen moved toward the ramshackle old house.

"Good God, Ver," said Harry, "Renfrew'll do the whole place in shades of yellow!" Kevin Renfrew was known for always wearing yellow. He said it brought sunshine into even the dullest day. Verderan's wife, Emily, had christened him the Daffodil Dandy.

"More than likely," said Verderan urbanely. "It should brighten this part of Leicestershire considerably."

They entered the house through a side door into a moldering estate room and passed into the dingy hall. There they encountered Emily Templemore.

Her ready smile was wide and warm. "Oh good," she said. "Guests."

She came to stand by her husband, and he wrapped an arm around her waist. "Just what we need, yes?" he said. He looked down at her and his friendly smile became something much deeper, which she echoed. "We're three months married and life's becoming tedious. We've only Randal, Sophie, and Renfrew here to amuse us in the evenings." Verderan looked up at the three. "I do hope you have some enlivening activity to share with us."

"Randal's back?" said Harry. "Good."

"We might," said Chart, with a sliding, puckish look at Harry. "Know anything of the de Lacys of Stonycourt?"

Later that night, as they prepared for bed, Harry said to Chart, "I'll thank you to keep your fingers out of my business!"

"So it is your business, is it?" queried Chart. He looked at his clothes. "I don't know why I gave Quincy the month off. My wardrobe is degenerating into rags."

"Pick 'em up," said Harry unsympathetically as he folded his own clothes. "You're not as useless as you make out."

With a smile, Chart obeyed. Hume house was not large, and some rooms were so neglected as to be undesirable, and so Corny was sharing with Kevin Renfrew while Harry and Chart shared this chamber.

As Chart folded his clothes he produced, as if by magic, a soiled rag. "Now, what is this?" he asked of no one in particular. He unfurled it, and it was clearly a lady's shift. He waved it in the manner of a matador with a cape.

Harry made a grab for it. Chart dodged. They tumbled to the floor and soon it was a full-fledged wrestling match.

In the end they cried quits and lay back in exhausted satisfaction. Harry looked for the source of contention and found it torn in two. It seemed a shame.

Chart sat up, arms around knees. "Care to tell me?"

Harry balled the rag up. "It's not what you think."

"What do I think?"

"That Miss de Lacy and I had a pleasant romp while the storm raged."

"I don't think that."

Harry looked at him. "You don't?"

"She didn't have the look of a well-pleasured lady, and you didn't look as bedazzled as I'd expect in such a case. But if you try to tell me that tale again of her skulking out in the barn until the rain stopped, I'll call you a liar."

Harry tossed the ball of cloth into a corner. "She came in for help. She was like a drowned rat and covered head to toe in mud. We had to get her out of those wet clothes."

"Oh-ho!" Chart chortled.

Harry waved a warning fist in his face. "*She* got herself out of her wet clothes while I saw to that sorry excuse for a horse." He rose and went to put more coal on the fire. "When I came back she was wrapped in a blanket and a couple of towels." He turned to look at his friend. "Have you ever seen such a beauty?"

"No," said Chart simply.

Harry frowned. "Do you feel at all interested in wooing her?"

Chart got to his feet in amazement. "*Wooing her*? God, no. I could sit and look at her now and then, as I'd look at a piece of sculpture." He studied his friend in concern. "Not thinking of doing something stupid, are you?"

The moment had come.

Harry had found an opportunity to speak to his cousin Randal and had his feelings confirmed. It was more likely that his parents were downplaying the seriousness of the situation than exaggerating it, and in that case it would undoubtedly be best for him to put their minds at rest by marrying and setting up his nursery.

After meeting Amy de Lacy and spending an evening with Randal and his wife Sophie, and Verderan and Emily, the notion was no longer so intolerable.

The Ashbys and the Templemores were loving couples in very different ways. Randal and Sophie had married in August but it hadn't, as some had hoped, sobered them. They still treated life as a delightful game, but it was now a game they played as a team.

Verderan and Emily had married just before Christmas and disappeared for a long honeymoon. They had only been back a month and Harry had seen little of them in that time. He was amazed at the change Piers Verderan. No, not really a change, merely a heightening of his virtues and a marked diminution of his vices. His tongue was noticeably less sharp and his notorious temper seemed nonexistent.

Emily Templemore was not a Sophie. She was eight years older and of a much quieter disposition. She and Verderan loved in a quieter, more subtle way, and yet their love was as clear in the air as the perfume of roses.

Harry remembered Emily Grantwich in the days before she and Verderan had sorted out their affairs. She'd been weighed down by concerns, mostly to do with family. It seemed to him Amy de Lacy was similarly burdened. Was it possible he could bring a glow to Amy's eyes like the glow in Emily's?

Chart was looking at him with horror.

"My father's ill," Harry said. "He wants me to go to London and find a bride."

"Lord," said Chart, looking for all the world as if he'd just been told his friend had a fatal disease.

"It's not that bad," said Harry with a wry smile. "Look at Randal and Ver."

"They're six years older," Chart pointed out. "I've no mind to be tied down just yet."

"You don't have to. You've got a healthy father and a younger brother. And you don't have a title to carry on."

"Much to my father's disgust," said Chart. "So you're really going to do it? Almack's, the lot?"

Harry grinned. "Perhaps not." At Chart's look he said, "Amy de Lacy."

Chart frowned. "Are you sure that's wise? After all, what do you know of her other than that she's a raving beauty?"

Harry walked over and got into bed. "We did talk," he pointed out.

Chart extinguished the candles and joined him. "And?"

"She's easy to talk to. She has a sense of humor. She's very sensible. After all, Chart, most girls would have thrown fits to be in such a state, and would probably have rather frozen to death than done the sensible thing and take off their clothes."

Chart was lying back with his hands behind his head. He chuckled. "True enough. Remarkable just how reluctant most females are to strip down, no matter how sensible it might be." He sobered. "Don't bite my head off, old man, but are you sure she didn't hope for something more than talk?"

Harry leaned up on one elbow. "I'm sure. She was in a fine state of nerves."

"Quite reasonably if she'd set out to seduce you. I will

credit her with being a virgin. Emily said her family's all rolled up. It wouldn't be surprising if a beauty like that decided to catch herself a good husband by unconventional means." He looked at his friend. "Going five miles for some broody hens sounds a bit rum to me."

Harry leaned back. He didn't like Chart's words, but he had to admit there was some sense to them. "She could hardly have planned the storm. No one expected it."

"True, but she could have planned a broken rein. Look at it logically. She sets out to go five miles for something she could have got closer to home. She'd dressed in a smart gown when they're apparently impoverished. Did you notice that Emily said the beautiful Miss de Lacy is in the habit of wearing extremely dull, unornamented garments?"

"I noticed," said Harry.

"There was a bonnet in the box," Chart added, rather apologetically.

"What?"

"In the box of the dogcart. There was a very smart bonnet—blue silk lining, striped ribbons, the lot. I'll go odds she would have looked very fetching in it."

Harry sighed. The fire crackled. Far off in the hall, the old clock wheezed its way through the twelve strokes of midnight. "It doesn't matter," said Harry at last. "I don't blame her for trying to catch the interest of an eligible *parti*. After all, life must be miserable if they're as poor as it would appear, especially with some idiot insisting they live like the workhouse poor until they're out of debt. Doubtless that fusby-faced sister."

Chart shrugged. "As you will. Just as long as you're forewarned. Beauty's a damned dangerous thing, and once you swallow the bait you'll have the whole family on your hands." He rolled over and settled himself for sleep. "One good thing. If you can fix it all with Miss de Lacy, you won't have to do the Season. I'd probably think friendship required me to tag along and guard you from your better nature."

# === 6 ===

THE NEXT DAY, Chart and Harry announced their intention of riding over to Stonycourt to inquire after Miss de Lacy's welfare. Corny declined to accompany them, saying he had become quite interested in Kevin Renfrew's plans for Hume House. It was more a case, they knew, of him not being one for the ladies. Emily gave them a basket of food to take over with her compliments, instructing them to be sure to give it tactfully.

Later, as they trotted down the drive to Stonycourt, Harry said, "This is a fine property. Surprised someone could run himself into the ground with this."

"Mortgages," suggested Chart. "Gambling more than likely. Things like that," he pointed out, "run in families."

Harry gave him a disgusted look and speeded up, eager to see Amy de Lacy again. Would she be the warm, unconventional delight of the kitchen, or the cool young lady who had fobbed them off so efficiently yesterday?

And why, he wondered, had she turned frosty? It could have been a delayed attack of missishness, but he did not judge that to be in character. Perhaps it was maidenly shyness in the faces of her own warm feelings.

Chart's voice broke into his reverie. "I'd ask why you had a besotted grin on your face if I felt I really wanted to know."

Harry just grinned at him. After all, duty and inclination were coming together in a most satisfactory way, and he felt sorry for Chart, who clearly had no notion of the delights of falling comfortably in love.

They dismounted in front of the house, and when no groom appeared, tethered their horses. Harry went up the three shallow steps and rapped the knocker. Nothing happened. He rapped again.

He had his hand up to try a third time when the door swung open and Amy de Lacy stared at him, rendering him speechless.

He'd forgotten just how beautiful she was.

She was wearing a plain gown the color of weak, milky tea, largely covered by a black apron. There was a smudge of dirt across her cheek, and her gilded curls were an untamed riot with a cobweb draped across one side.

She was exquisite.

"Oh," she said. A hand fluttered to her hair and was restrained.

Harry gathered his wits and bowed. "Good morning, Miss de Lacy. Mr. Ashby and I came to see if you had recovered from your ordeal." He was aware of Chart beside him, tipping his hat.

She just stared at them with those mesmerizing blue eyes, and Harry felt like bursting into a chorus of Tom Moore's latest ditty. "The light that lies in women's eyes/ Has been my heart's undoing."

"Why, it's Mr. Crisp and Mr. Ashby." The welcome came not from Amy de Lacy but from her plain sister. "How lovely of you to call. Do please come in."

Harry bludgeoned his wits into order, tore his eyes away from his beloved, and managed to greet Miss de Lacy civilly.

Amy allowed Beryl to take over, though she knew she should forbid them the house. But how?

She'd been frozen, panicked by the flash of searing excitement which had jumped through her at the sight of him. She'd wanted to slam the door in his face and yet had known that was impossible. Now she wanted to run and hide in her room until he left.

"We are rather busy," she said.

A beaming Beryl was already shepherding them into the little-used and chilly drawing room. "You will stay for tea, won't you, Mr. Crisp, Mr. Ashby?"

"We'd be delighted," said Chart Ashby with a quizzical look at Amy. "Perhaps we can make a contribution." He proffered the basket. "Lady Templemore, our hostess, insisted in sending an invalid basket. I can see Miss de Lacy is recovered, but can I hope you will make use of it anyway? Lady Templemore will be hurt otherwise."

"Oh, how kind," said Beryl. She glanced at Amy for guidance, but Amy was too swamped by personal problems to worry about unwelcome charity. Beryl reached for the basket with enthusiasm.

Chart Ashby held on to it. "It is a trifle heavy," he said. "Perhaps I should carry it for you." He cast a meaningful glance at Harry and Amy.

"Oh yes!" declared Beryl, who'd just helped Amy move wardrobes as they did the spring cleaning. "That would be so kind." She quickly led the way to the kitchens.

Amy looked around and realized she was alone with Harry Crisp. "Oh dear."

"My dear Miss de Lacy," Harry said with a teasing smile, "you are surely not nervous to be alone with me. We've weathered worse than this after all, and the door is safely open."

Amy could feel her cheeks heat. She found herself fiddling with her apron and stopped. "Yes," she said. "I mean we have, and I'm not . . ." This would never do. She wished he weren't here. She wished the room weren't so shabby. She wished she were still the wealthy Amy de Lacy, dressed in modish style and receiving a handsome gentlemen without thought of her duty to marry riches.

She realized she was still in her work apron and pulled it off. Then, unsure what to do with it, she tucked it under a cushion. "It is a lovely day, isn't it? I do hope you had a pleasant ride."

He was looking at her with warm amusement and considerable tenderness. It was as if they were back at

Coppice Farm. Her anxiety melted away and she laughed. "That was ridiculous, wasn't it? I don't know why I should be ashamed to be seen in an apron when the whole world knows we have to do for ourselves. Won't you be seated, Mr. Crisp."

She took a straight-back chair and he took another close beside it.

"We are all driven by convention," Harry said. "I don't think the worse of you for having to do menial work. But I think it a shame."

Amy smiled ruefully and looked down at her hands—not ruined yet, but rougher than they used to be. "So do I, but then I think that there's no reason I should be exempt. Why should one woman heave furniture and another idle her days away?"

"Is that what you've been doing?" he asked, startled. He picked up her right hand and studied it with a frown, tracing a line of dirt with one finger.

Amy tried to pull away. "I must go and wash."

He held on. "That doesn't matter. But you do have servants," he said. "I surely saw one yesterday."

He continued to hold her hand, and the warmth of his skin against hers was . . . distracting. "Pretty and Mrs. Pretty," she said unsteadily. "But they are more pensioners than servants. They have worked at Stonycourt all their lives and deserve a pension." His thumb was rubbing against her skin. "There's . . . there's no money to pay for it. So they live on here. It's that or the . . . the workhouse. Please let me go!"

"Why?" he asked.

Amy could have cited propriety but instead she said weakly, "My hands are so dirty."

"I don't mind," he said and raised her hand for a kiss. Then he released it.

She was a regular Cinderella, Harry thought, having to struggle not to show his anger at her lazy servants and her ugly sister. More than ever he wanted to sweep her into his arms, kiss her, and carry her off to Hey Park, where she could idle her days away in peace.

She leapt to her feet and moved away from him. How shy she was. "Jasper and Jassy help," she carried on. "But Jasper is at school most of the time—he boards at Uppingham—and Jassy has her lessons, too. Aunt Lizzie does a great deal of the cooking, but she's too old to do heavy work."

"You're too delicate to do heavy work," Harry said firmly.

She turned to him in surprise. "I'm not the slightest bit delicate," she said. "You mustn't be deceived by my appearance." She walked over and picked up a sturdy chair, raising it above her head. By the time he was on his feet to assist her, she had already set it down again. "See?"

"So you're a female Atlas," he snapped, filled again with a burning desire to claim her and put an end to such foolishness. "That doesn't mean you should be doing such things."

"Rooms need to be cleaned," she pointed out, "and that means furniture must be moved. So, we move it."

"This is all nonsense," he said. "You may be in straightened circumstances, Miss de Lacy, but this degree of hardship cannot be necessary. You are being shamefully ill used."

"By whom?" she asked, appearing to be genuinely at loss. She was such an innocent darling.

He hesitated to name her hard-hearted family since she seemed devoted to them, but he had noticed that the sister had been wearing quite a tolerable green spring muslin while Amy was in little more than a rag.

He was saved when Beryl bustled into the room, followed by Chart Ashby bearing the tray, and an older lady carrying a plate of cakes. A cruel aunt instead of a stepmother.

"Tea!" the older woman declared with a degree of emphasis which seemed uncalled for.

They all sat as tea and cake were dispensed. Chart noticed that both the sister and the aunt raised their cups to their lips as if the china contained a sacred beverage. After the first taste they sighed softly in unison. He glanced at Amy, but she held her cup and saucer forgotten in her hands.

"Do you not care for tea, Miss Amy?" he asked.

She started and looked down. "Oh, yes." She sipped and then smiled. "It is good, isn't it?"

It occurred to him at last they perhaps were not able to afford tea. True, it was expensive, particularly since the war, and was always kept in a locked caddy, but he'd never known anyone before who could not afford it. Even the tenants at Hey Park would have an ounce or two in a tin for the occasional cup.

A proposal hovered on his lips. He could put an end to this here and now—provide tea, wine, and good food; dress Amy as befitted her station; and hire servants so she ceased such foolish, dangerous activities. But she deserved better than such a hurly-burly offer.

He realized Chart was adroitly holding up their end of the conversation and began to take part himself. The sister and aunt were less honest than Amy and attempted to keep up appearances, but he still gathered a bleak picture of their situation. He couldn't help but wonder if they would be better advised to sell up and live in modest comfort, but it would be time to look into such things when he was part of the family. They were obviously in need of proper advice. The new baronet was a mere schoolboy, and the trustee lived in Cumberland and paid little attention to their affairs. Harry gathered he was a poet of sorts.

He'd bring in his father's man-of-business and the Hey Park steward to assess the situation and decide what should be done for the best.

Amy relished her tea, even though she knew this whole event was a disaster. It was as Beryl had said; it would be so much harder to go back to herbs after savoring bohea. Moreover, Beryl and Aunt Lizzie were enjoying this little party so much that they would stretch it out as long as possible, when Amy knew she needed to have Harry Crisp leave.

She just couldn't seem to stay sensible, especially when he touched her.

She recognized the warning signs. Yesterday he may

have treated her as a brother—for most of the time, anyway—but today he had a different look in his eye. If she wasn't very careful he would propose to her, and she didn't want to have to hurt him by a refusal. To worry her more, there was always the danger that she wouldn't manage to refuse him at all.

If he were to touch her, perhaps kiss her . . .

"Amy!"

Amy looked up suddenly and would have spilled the tea if there had been any left in the cup.

"What were you about?" Beryl asked. "It looked as if you were trying to read your future in the leaves."

They had played that game in the good old days. She grinned and peered into the cup. "Let's see. Goodness, I have a very twisty road here. Life is going to be complicated in the future, I fear. But I have a tree. That," she said with a flashing look at Harry, "means sturdy good health."

He leaned over to look. "How can you see a tree in all that? It's just a splattering of tea leaves."

"Oh ye of little faith. *I* can see a tree. And a road."

"And what of marriage?" he asked lightly. "Is that not what all young ladies seek in the leaves?"

Amy realized she had allowed herself to slide into warmth again and drew back, but he had his hand on her cup and she could not retreat far without a struggle. "A ring signifies marriage," she said.

He looked and then smiled at her. "I see a very clear ring."

"Oh, Amy," declared Beryl. "How lovely!"

"It is marred by a cross," countered Amy.

Beryl's face fell. "Oh dear."

Harry shared an indulgent glance with Chart Ashby. "And what does that mean?"

"It means," said Beryl seriously, "that Amy will experience many difficulties before she marries and is in danger of failing to find true love there."

Harry glanced into the cup again and then surrendered it to Amy. "I hope I do not offend, ladies, but I don't think that is a good prediction of Miss Amy's future at all." It was time for them to take their leave, and with some reluctance he led the way.

As they rode off he turned to Chart. "Well?"

Chart shrugged. "I don't know. She seems charming enough. I suppose you could do worse. I suspect she'll want you to lay out a lot of blunt on the place."

"My father won't mind helping them out, providing some comforts. As to the estate, we'll have to see if there's anything to save. They seem to be in desperate straights."

They discussed estate management on the way back in a competent manner which would have surprised and delighted their parents.

Back at Hume House, Harry announced his intention of asking Amy de Lacy to marry him as soon as it seemed appropriate, and was pleased to find that no one had any objection to raise.

Amy tried to put Harry Crisp out of her mind, which wasn't easy when Beryl and Lizzie dwelt on the visit all the time. Jassy, returning from yet another visit to Amabelle's, was put out to find she had missed the beaux, and so she stayed at home the next day.

"They won't call again," said Amy.

"Who?" asked Jassy innocently.

"The king and queen," Amy retorted. "But if you think we might have visitors, make yourself useful and dust the drawing room."

Aunt Lizzie, she noticed, was polishing the tiles in the front hall, and Beryl had gone out to look for flowers—both in their best gowns. Amy shook her head and went off in her workaday brown bombazine to take the kitchen scraps to the pig.

This was her latest project. After all, most of the tenants had a pig. Augustus would survive almost entirely on scraps and then, come winter, provide bacon, ham, and sausage.

As she tipped out the bucket for the eager fellow with

his comical flapping ears, Amy wished Jassy hadn't christened him. She scratched him behind one ear as he snuffled around for the choice bits. "How are you, then, Augustus?" she asked. "That's right. Eat up. I don't suppose it will help when the time comes, but I'll make sure you're as happy as possible until then."

Augustus looked up and gave a strange little snort of disbelief. "Oh dear," said Amy.

"Do you always talk to the livestock?"

She whirled around to find herself face to face with Harry Crisp. "What on earth are you doing, creeping up on me like that!"

He looked down at his top boots. "I don't think it's possible to creep in boots on a gravel path, Miss de Lacy. I think it was more a case of you being enthralled by your companion."

"Nonsense," said Amy, face flaming. "I was merely feeding him. Fattening him up. They . . . er . . . feed better when talked to."

Harry looked over the sty wall. "He seems to be eating well still."

"Because of the sound of human voices," said Amy triumphantly.

Harry leaned against the wall and grinned at her. "Then I suppose it is our duty to stay here and talk."

Amy picked up the bucket. "I have work to do."

He took the bucket from her and held her hand. "The lowest laborer is entitled to a rest." He looked over the sty wall again. "I see you were correct. The poor pig has stopped eating. We must talk more."

Amy looked down and saw he was telling the truth. Augustus was not rooting in the trough but looking up longingly. She knew it was not foolishness, but his expectation of the treat she always brought in her pocket and gave before she left—an apple, a carrot, sometimes a piece of leftover pie or stale cake. Today, because of Lady Templemore's bounty, she'd stolen a buttered scone for him.

"I was fooling," she said. "I could recite *The Corsair* and make no difference to his eating."

Augustus rested his snout against the top of the wall and squealed demandingly.

"He protests that. *Can* you recite the *The Corsair*?"

"Of course not. I doubt even Lord Byron can."

"Perhaps you should just relate the story of your life," he suggested with a smile. "For the pig's sake, of course."

Amy gave him a disgusted look. "Augustus couldn't care a fig for my history." She pulled out the scone. "This what he wants." She tossed it into the sty. The pig gave a snort that said, About time, too, gulped it down, and went back to eating.

"You see," said Amy. "Just like all males. Cupboard love." She walked briskly back toward the house and he kept pace with her, the bucket clattering against his leg.

"Do you really have such a low opinion of men?" he asked.

Amy regretted her tartness. She slowed her pace and said, "I'll have to hope it's not true. My cupboard, after all, is bare."

He put down the bucket and stopped her with a hand on her arm. "Hardly that, Miss de Lacy. There are other riches than money."

*Oh dear. I've forgotten to be careful and we're in trouble again.* "If you mean my beauty," she said prosaically, "I have no desire to be married for looks. What would become of me in a few years when they fade?" *And yet that is what I plan to do.*

She pulled against his hand, but he merely brought his other hand to her other arm to hold her more firmly. "I shan't let you run away just yet. You know you have nothing to fear from me."

*Oh no I don't.*

"I don't deny that you have beauty, Miss de Lacy, but you also have courage, honesty, and a warm heart. It extends," he said with a smile, "even to the porker. May I hope it extends to me?"

Amy could feel panic growing in her. It would be so easy, so wonderful, to say yes. He would make her happy. He would give Beryl and Jassy and even Lizzie a comfortable home, perhaps even give her sisters a small dowry each. He would help Jasper, and after all, it would not be so terrible to lose some land, and some of the silver and pictures. . . .

"Miss de Lacy?" he prompted. "Amy?"

But it would be utter selfishness. She would be the only one to benefit when she could provide everything that was required. "I am grateful to you, of course," she said woodenly.

"You know that isn't what I mean," he said gently. "Amy, will you marry me?"

Amy stopped breathing. She knew that because she noticed when she needed breath to say, "No."

Color touched his cheeks. "A bit abrupt," he remarked. "Could you give me a reason? I'm healthy, wealthy, and willing. Where lies my shortcoming?"

Amy swallowed and took refuge in the banal. "We hardly know each other, sir."

Foolishness was always unwise. "I feel I know you better than any number of young women I've danced with, and walked with, and been acquainted with for years."

"I don't know you at all," Amy persisted.

"Don't you?" he queried. "Well then, have I your permission to visit you, so that you may get to know me better?"

She was hurting him. She hated this. But it was unfair of him to badger her so. "I don't think so."

"Miss de Lacy," he said with a touch of impatience, "if you have taken me in dislike, or if you are already pledged to another, I wish you would tell me directly. Otherwise, these dillydallyings of yours are very strange."

At this reproof, Amy applied all her strength and wrenched herself out of his hands. "Strange?" she echoed. "I always thought a man was supposed to take no for an answer, sir. Instead, you're hounding me to death. Two days ago we were total strangers." She raked her hands distractedly through her hair. "Why on earth *would* I want to marry you?"

"Because I can rescue you from poverty, if nothing else," he said, looking every bit as distraught as she. "You may not be ready to agree to marry me now, Miss de Lacy, but you have no reason to dismiss me out of hand, unless your beauty has so gone to your head that you are holding out for a better catch. I think I am entitled to a logical reason for your refusal to even consider my suit."

Amy welcomed the rare surge of temper, for it swamped the pain. She hissed in a breath through her teeth. "Very well, sir," she snapped. "If you want logic, you may have it!" She looked him straight in the eye. "I *am* holding out for a better catch. I plan to marry a fortune, and you are nowhere near rich enough." She laughed at the shock on his face. "I could be wrong, of course, our acquaintance being so slight as to be nonexistent. If you are a regular Croesus, pray tell me now and I'll say yes, and thank you, sir, and be as grovelingly grateful as you clearly expect me to be."

"I do not—"

She interrupted him. "But you're not a Croesus, are you? And so you're no use to me, Mr. Crisp, for all that you're a handsome, pleasant young man. I intend to marry only an immensely rich man."

He turned white. "You bitch."

At the end of her tether, Amy hit him, knocking his head sideways with the force of it. The sound cracked, and in seconds the scarlet mark was on his face like a red flag. Manual labor developed the muscles remarkably.

"Amethyst!" gasped Aunt Lizzie.

Amy turned, horrified, to see Aunt Lizzie, Beryl, Jassy, and Chart Ashby gaping at her. She wished the earth would swallow her. How had she ever become so lost to proper behavior? She turned, seeking adequate apologetic words.

Harry laughed in her face. "I should have known," he said. "Even your name is false. You're not an Amy, you're an Amethyst—beautiful, cold, hard. And for sale to the highest bidder."

Amy forgot apologies. "Leave!" she commanded and

pointed dramatically toward the distant gates. "And you will never be welcome here again."

Harry looked her over. "There is certainly nothing here to tempt me." He bowed curtly to the other ladies and stalked off.

Everyone simply stood frozen.

After a moment Chart Ashby made an elegant bow. "Apologies, ladies. 'Fraid we'll have to miss our dish of tea."

No one said a word as he followed his friend, but then Aunt Lizzie said, "Amethyst . . ."

Amy burst into tears and fled to her room.

When Chart arrived at the drive where they had left their horses, Harry was already at the end of the drive, heading away from Stonycourt at a gallop. Chart made no hurry about following. A long, blistering, lonely ride was probably what his friend needed right now.

# = 7 =

CHART SAW NO SIGN of Harry during the leisurely canter back to Hume House. That didn't surprise him. If he'd been assaulted by his beloved, he'd doubtless disappear to lick his wounds.

Chart was mildly puzzled over the behavior of the beautiful Amethyst. Harry Crisp would be quite a catch for her, so why the furor? He couldn't imagine that Harry had done or said anything to truly warrant such outrage. That wasn't in Harry's style. Too sweet-natured for his own good, was Harry, and especially gentle with ladies of all degrees.

When he strolled into Hume House he expected inquiries as to Harry's whereabouts. Instead he was greeted with, "What's got into Harry?"

They were all in what passed for a drawing room—Verderan, Emily, Randal, Sophie, Corny, and Renfrew. It was Randal who had spoken. He was a spectacularly handsome man with golden curls and bright blue eyes made for teasing. In their schooldays he'd been the Bright Angel to Verderan's Dark, but he had left the nickname behind.

"Why d'you ask?" Chart replied.

"Because he stormed in here like a Fury," Randal said, "grabbed a decanter of brandy, and headed for your room. There was a crash a while back but it didn't sound fatal."

"Lord," said Chart, rather awed. He tried to remember

the last time Harry had lost his temper. He didn't think Harry ever had.

"He can wreck the place if he wants," said Verderan. "I'm sure there's nothing of value. But we'd rather not have a corpse in the house."

"What happened?" asked Randal seriously.

"I'm not sure," said Chart. "We rode over, and when we spotted the beautiful Amy in the kitchen garden Harry went over to do a spot of wooing while I went up to the house. The other ladies fussed and prepared tea, but when Harry and his beloved didn't come in we all went to find them. We came upon them on the path in a grand heat. He called her a bitch. She hit him and ordered him off the estate. He seemed to be in a taking because her name's Amethyst. I don't know why."

"Amethyst," said Emily. "I only ever heard her called Amy, but it makes sense. They're all named for stones."

"Beautiful, cold, hard, and for sale to the highest bidder," said Chart. "That's a quotation."

"Harry?" queried Randal in amazement.

"Harry."

Everyone in the room took time to ponder this. They all knew Harry Crisp to be an equable young man with beautiful manners.

Kevin Renfrew said, "There speaks a man in love." He appeared completely serious and everyone took it that way. Renfrew had a gift of seeing the best and the truth in everyone.

"In that case," said Verderan dryly, "I think we should give him a few pointers on a more subtle wooing technique."

"Ha!" scoffed Emily. "Who's claiming to be an expert? As I understand it, Sophie had to woo Randal, and you just teased me to death."

"At least you never hit me," he responded with a smile.

"I tried at least once. You were just too quick for me."

"Then perhaps we should teach Harry that, too." He kissed her hand and sobered. "I think someone should go up and make sure he isn't putting a pistol to his head. Volunteers?"

"He wouldn't," protested Chart. "Over a woman?"

Randal got to his feet. "You obviously lack all sympathy with pangs of the heart. And it should be kept in the family. I'll go."

Randal knocked on the door. When there was no answer, he opened it and walked in. Harry was sitting by the window, staring out. The crash had obviously been the decanter which lay shattered in a corner. From the size of the puddle and the strength of the fumes, very little if any had been drunk.

"You prefer to inhale your solace, do you?" said Randal.

Harry didn't turn. "It's all right. I'm neither going to drink myself to death nor shoot myself. Not over a heartless, deceiving bitch."

Randal closed the door. "I'm more concerned that you might walk out and offer for the first woman you see, just to prove how little this one means to you."

Harry did turn at that, sharply. "She means nothing. We only met two days ago."

Randal went to lounge in a chair. "There seems a remarkable amount of heat for such a brief acquaintance. As a senior member of the family, I have to ask. Did you dishonor her yesterday?"

"No," said Harry sharply, color returning to his cheeks.

"But today you asked her to marry you."

"Yes."

"And she said no."

"Yes."

Randal steepled his fingers and considered his cousin. "How did such a simple discussion come to blows?"

Harry got to his feet. "That's none of your damn business. There's no cause for concern. I'm not a danger to myself or anyone else. I will doubtless never set eyes on the alluring Amethyst again, for which I am immensely grateful." He flung open the window. "Best get rid of these fumes before night, or we'll go to bed sober and rise drunk."

Randal shrugged and got to his feet. "What are your plans, then?"

"Hunting's just about over," Harry said. "I suppose I'll visit my parents then settle myself in Town. Run my eye over the latest crop of fillies," he said callously, "and pick the one that takes my fancy most. Might as well go for a handsome portion while I'm at it, I suppose. Any younger children will thank me." He looked at Randal with a slight, humorless smile. "That's how it's done, ain't it?"

"Oh, surely," said Randal dryly. "And be sure to check the soundness of her teeth and the width of her hips." He went to the door. "Are you leaving tomorrow, then?"

"Why not?"

"Why not indeed." With that Randal left and went thoughtfully downstairs. There he related most of the conversation to the others.

Chart groaned. "That means I'll have to do all that social nonsense, too."

"Excellent idea," said Randal. "He needs a close eye kept on him. In fact," he said with a smile at his wife, "I think the Season calls us too."

"Oh good," said Sophie with a brilliant smile. "I'll be able to show off my prize."

"My thought entirely," said Randal and wound one of her auburn curls around his finger.

Verderan said, "Tempting though it is, I think we will give this circus a miss." He took Emily's hand and kissed it. "I have yet to show Emily my principal estate and we intend to live quietly for a while. It is near London, however, on the river near Putney. You will be welcome if you decide you need some country air." He smiled around. "If you wonder why we are settled on bucolic idleness, it is because by next year, there will be three Verderans in the family."

The meeting turned to celebratory drinks.

Chart found the claret soothing, and he began to take a brighter view of the future. He'd always had a bad feeling about Amy de Lacy, and Harry was well rid of her. When he bethought himself that the final defeat of

Napoleon Bonaparte was likely to turn the Season of 1814 into a gala affair, Chart was actually beginning to look forward to the adventure. Until Randal took him apart.

"Chart, since you're likely to be the man on the spot, keep a close eye on him."

"He won't do anything silly," said Chart. "He's seen that woman for what she is."

"Perhaps. There may, however, be a natural tendency to offer for the first tolerable woman he sets eyes on. Not a good idea."

"No?"

"No."

"And I'm supposed to stop him?"

"I'm sure you're up to the task."

On the whole, Chart thought, the next few months were going to be hell.

If Amy had known of these sentiments, she would have echoed them.

Her family were horrified with her. Not only had she been intolerably vulgar, she also had summarily disposed of two handsome, comfortably circumstanced young bachelors.

"And after all, dear Amethyst," said Aunt Lizzie at the end of one of her daily laments, "even in the tediously mercenary standards you seem to have espoused, you might have thought that a bird in the hand is worth two in the bush and kept him dangling. Then, if it turned out that you did not want him, Beryl and Jassy would have had a chance."

The Prettys were the only ones who seemed to approve. "You can do better than a stripling like that, Miss Amy," mumbled Mrs. Pretty around a mouthful of loose teeth. "You go after that Mr. Staverley again. He's a warm man and no mistake, and in control of his own."

Amy, desperate to prove to her family that she could rescue something from the debacle, set out to do just this. She pondered a number of fanciful plans, but the fact was that she couldn't take to haunting a spot five miles away from Stonycourt without causing talk.

The first trip to get the layers had in fact been plausible, and Amy repeated it two days after her disgrace. She lacked the nerve to stage some kind of accident as she passed the gates of Prior's Grange on the way to Hetty Cranby's. She told herself she would think of a good excuse on the way back. Perhaps she could fray the reins again.

But Hetty Cranby made it clear the whole area knew of her misadventure—the edited version, at least—courtesy of the Coneybears. Another idèntical accident so close by would be bound to set people thinking. Any accident at all would be suspicious. Amy drove back past the solid, prosperous, newly painted gates of the Grange and gave a wistful sigh.

She had to pass Coppice Farm both coming and going, but she encouraged herself with the knowledge that the inhabitants were far away. As she passed it on the return journey, however, she remembered that she had left her ruined shift there. It was presumably just lying in the kitchen, since the three young men no longer had a servant and were hardly likely to tidy the place themselves.

She pulled Zephyr up. What she ought to do was go in and retrieve it before someone else came across it. With her story buzzing around the area, and *A de L* embroidered upon it, someone would be sure to put two and two together.

It was the last thing she wanted to do, but she pulled into the yard. She sat there, listening, wondering what she would do if, by some terrible mischance, Harry Crisp came out to see who the visitor was. The local grapevine had been definite that all three young men had left the area the day after that horrible meeting, but the grapevine could be wrong.

She found she was actually shivering with nerves.

The place was clearly deserted, however. It was silent, and there was no smoke rising from the chimney.

Amy climbed down and went to knock timidly at the

door. Then she knocked more firmly. When there was no answer, she lifted the latch and went in.

The building had the dead feel of a house left empty for some time and it was as she had thought—little attempt had been made to clean up. The trail of mud down the passageway and into the kitchen was still there like a ghostly memory of her adventure. There was the tub in which she'd washed the dress. There was the dried mark of the muddy puddle they'd made when wringing it.

Realizing she was just standing here, where she would hate to be discovered, Amy hurried to the hearth where she had dropped the garment. There was no sign of it. She checked all around the room but it simply was not there. Growing frantic, she searched the scullery and the yard outside the scullery door, in case it had been thrown away.

It was nowhere to be found.

Amy took a deep, steadying breath. Could she hope that he'd burnt it?

Why would he do that?

She checked the cold ashes in the grate but they could tell her nothing. She hunted through the room again, hopelessly but driven.

What if he'd taken it?

What could he do with it?

She'd heard tales of young rascals laying bets on a lady's dishonor and producing an intimate garment as proof. Despite the warm sunshine, she shivered and hugged herself. Surely Harry Crisp wouldn't do such a thing.

From their first meeting, she would never have thought so, but now . . . she'd hurt and offended him. She shuddered when she remembered the way he'd said, "You bitch." How those warm brown eyes had turned hard and cold. She'd never imagined a man saying such a terrible thing to her, but he was right. She was the lowest of the low, a fortune hunter.

She looked at the plain, bare table and saw an oily stain where the automaton had stood.

Lady Jane was gone, of course. Amy remembered his long, sensitive fingers trying to mend the doll. Remembered the way he had made her feel as he ran his hands up the doll's fragile leg. How he had made her feel when he had touched her skin.

That man would never unjustly ruin a lady any more than he would smash that delicate toy. But the man she had made with her cruel words might.

With a last, sad look around at the dismal remnants of the magical afternoon, Amy left Coppice Farm.

It was Pretty who dug up the information which enabled Amy to make her next foray after Staverley.

He came sidling up one day as Amy was scrubbing the family wash in the huge tub. "Don't do that, don't," he said. "Ruin your hands, that will."

"Volunteering?" asked Amy wearily. Her patience with everyone was wearing thin.

"Rheumatics," he said by the way of excuse. "Got some news of that Staverley gent."

Amy looked up and brushed her hair back from her brow with a wet hand. At this moment, she felt too weary to become excited about her prey but she said, "What?"

"Grounds of Prior's Grange have some sort of old stone building. Everyone thought it was a croft or such like. Yon Mr. Staverley's taken it into his head it's part of the old monastery. He's setting to have it cleaned up so as to have his own real Gothic ruin. Very excited about it, he be. Probably like to share his interest."

Amy looked at the old man thoughtfully, then nodded. She left the clothes to soak and went in search of Beryl.

"We have developed a passionate interest in the Gothic," Amy told her.

"We have?" Beryl was engaged in making new slippers for Jassy.

"Yes, and you are going to write to Mr. Owen Staverley and ask his permission to visit the ruin on his estate and sketch it. We still have some sketching pads, do we not?"

"Yes, but . . ."

"And I will come with you."

Beryl put aside her work. "I don't know, Amy . . ."

"Come on, Beryl. You used to love sketching romantic ruins!"

Beryl smiled. "Well actually, I *would* like to see it, and before Mr. Staverley 'improves' it. He'll probably put a tower on it, or the like."

"Doubtless. It's as well you do have a genuine interest in such things. You'll have to prime me with clever questions and be prepared to interrupt if I run out of things to say. But after all," she said grimly, "I will only have to smile and look beautiful, won't I?"

She returned to the washing. Beryl considered her thoughtfully, slippers forgotten in her hands.

Thus it was that one morning in May, Amy and Beryl drove past Coppice Farm on their way to the Grange. Amy was intensely grateful that Beryl didn't realize the significance of the place.

Beryl had written a note and Mr. Staverley had responded quite warmly, encouraging them to visit and promising to show them the building himself. Amy wished she felt more uplifted now the moment was at hand, but at least she would be grateful to have it all done with.

Beryl was dressed in a very pleasing cream muslin, which looked as fine as could be because it was far too impractical to have been worn for housework. Amy had insisted on wearing the refurbished blue. If any mischance occurred, she didn't want to ruin another of Beryl's small stock of pretty gowns. In fact the blue cambric had turned out remarkably well dyed a deeper shade and with a striped flounce to hide the stains around the hem.

It was unfortunate that it held indelible memories.

On consideration, Amy had decided that she had overdone things last time, and so both she and Beryl wore their warm, red, hooded cloaks, universal everyday wear of ladies in the country. The cloaks lessened any impression that they might be dressed for effect.

When Zephyr plodded through the handsome gates and up the well-groomed drive to Prior's Grange, Beryl looked around at the smooth meadows and well-tended flowerbeds and said, "Oh, how pretty it is."

"Yes," said Amy sourly, for she was keyed up with nerves. "But that was never the Prior's Grange."

Beryl looked ahead at the house and chuckled. "Assuredly not." It was a slightly shrunken Palladian mansion, all white stone and pillars. "There was a monastery here, though, Amy, so presumably there was a grange. And as Mr. Staverley has just bought the place, he cannot be held responsible for the misnomer."

"He bought it," said Amy as they pulled up.

Beryl looked at her in concern. "If you have taken the place in dislike, you will not want to live here, love."

Amy forced a smile and laughed. "I haven't taken it in dislike. It is actually a pleasing house, with a slightly strange name. I promise, if this gentleman offers his hand and his heart, I won't hit him for his impudence."

Beryl looked worried, but Amy stalked up to the door and applied the gleaming knocker. This brought a footman, and Mr. Staverley hot on his heels.

He was not a prepossessing man. He was rather short in stature, but with a heavy chest and a head a little too large. His hair was a thinning brown, muted by gray, and his eyes were a very ordinary blue. His skin was darkly sallow, doubtless due to his years in a hot climate.

"You must be the Misses de Lacy," he said abruptly, not looking too pleased at the discovery.

As Beryl confirmed this and made a few conversational comments, Amy decided this plan wouldn't work either. Owen Staverley wasn't interested in them. He'd hand them over to a servant and that would be the end of it.

She couldn't be altogether sorry. She didn't want to marry this monkey of a man, but she remembered her task and steeled herself to do her best. When Beryl introduced her, she fixed on her face what she hoped was a demure smile and watched for any warmth or admiration in his eye.

He looked at her fixedly, blinked, then turned away without reaction or comment. "Come along, ladies. Let me show you the building in question. As you have an interest in these things, I'll welcome your opinion."

Amy sighed. So much for her reputation as a slayer of men. Even as a fortune hunter she was a sorry specimen.

Two hours later Amy was counting over all the useful things she could have done with this afternoon. She could have weeded the vegetable garden, mucked out Zephyr, washed some windows, taken down the winter curtains to put up the summer ones, patched her gray merino.

Heavens, she could have curled up by a window in the sun and read a book—a rare luxury these days.

Instead, she wandered around on Mr. Staverley's left as he conversed at length with Beryl on his right about monastic architecture. True, she had been given the opportunity to sketch the small stone hut, which was the center of interest, but though she was tolerably skilled at art she could make nothing inspiring of it. If it was a monastery chapel, she'd eat the drawing pad, board and all.

It was Beryl who somewhat hesitantly expressed these doubts, causing their surly host to frown even more.

"But I do think it may be an acolyte's cell, Mr. Staverley," Beryl quickly added. "That would be much more interesting, and could mean the building is older than you think. I am no authority, but it may even date as far back as the twelfth century."

"Twelfth century, eh?" he barked, and marched about a bit. "Hmm. Come back and drink some tea, ladies. We must discuss this further!"

Must we? thought Amy as she collected her materials and followed the other two. Her laggardly progress was not noticed.

Yet another man not obviously smitten by her charms. That made Martin Howgarth, Terance Cornwalis, Chart Ashby, and Mr. Staverley. And whatever he might once have thought, Harry Crisp surely wanted nothing to do with her anymore. Now that she needed her allure it seemed to have evaporated. Had it gone, or was it perhaps something that shone the brightest when she was trying to conceal it?

She had to consider this seriously, for since Mr. Staverley was not going oblige her with an offer, it would have to be London. The shocking expense involved meant that she *must* succeed. Should she dress with puritan simplicity and maintain a sober countenance, or should she deck herself out in fashion and simper?

"Amy, dear, is something the matter?"

Amy realized she had actually stopped still to ponder this, and her sister and Mr. Staverley were ahead on the path, waiting for her.

She hurried after them. "No, nothing at all," she said gaily. Feeling she had to offer some explanation she added, "I was just taken by the beauty of a bird song and had to stop and listen."

Mr. Staverley gave a kind of snort and hurried them on to the house like a bad-tempered sheepdog.

Once there he arranged for the housekeeper to take them to a room where they could wash their hands before tea.

"Well, Amy?" asked Beryl excitedly as soon as they were alone.

"Well what?" Amy replied shortly. "The man clearly is not interested."

"Oh, I'm sure he looked at you particularly a number of times!"

"Truly?" Amy couldn't be sure whether this was Beryl's wishful thinking or not.

"Truly." Beryl checked her hair in the glass. "You didn't seem to want to join in the discussion of the building, so it was doubtless difficult for him to express his interest. It will go better during tea, you'll see." She looked around the room. "Pretty was quite correct. Everything is of the best and in very good taste."

Except the owner, thought Amy, but she accompanied her sister back to the salon determined to do her duty if the opportunity should arise.

"Ah," said Mr. Staverley, in his abrupt way. "Tea in here as you see. You'll pour, Miss de Lacy."

Beryl looked as if she would defer to Amy but went to sit before the tray and dispense. Amy looked at the table laden with sandwiches and cakes and felt her spirits lift. At least something good would come out of this. She wondered if there was any possibility of smuggling some of the delicious fruitcake home for the others.

Beryl suddenly spoke in a loud voice. "My sister was remarking how handsome this house is, Mr. Staverley."

Amy remembered her duty. "Indeed yes, Mr. Staverley. An excellent property."

"Place was a mess when I bought it. Sold for debts. World's full of fools. Didn't even know that building was anything but a croft."

Within moments the conversation was firmly back on medieval architecture. Beryl flashed Amy an imperative glance, but Amy could think of nothing sensible to say. She failed to see how her talking like a fool would advance her cause. She devoted herself instead to looking interested and beautiful while she planned a slightly different arrangement of the kitchen garden, which might prove economical of time.

As soon as they were on their way home, she said, "That's that, then. It has to be London."

"He may just be shy, dearest," said Beryl.

"Shy!" scoffed Amy. "He doesn't know the meaning of the word. He's a bad-tempered, selfish man and I'm glad he isn't interested."

"Oh dear. I can't help but feel you are being harsh. I found him most intelligent and considerate. But if you have taken him in dislike, dearest, you assuredly must not consider marrying him for a moment."

"I could marry him for a moment," retorted Amy. "It's the 'till death do us part' bit that's daunting."

Hearing her own words, she burst out laughing and Beryl joined in. But it wasn't funny, Amy thought. Who was she going to have to tie herself to for the rest of her life?

A picture invaded of a tawny-haired young man with a fine strong body, and a mouth made for smiling. Romantical nonsense, she told herself firmly.

By then they were passing Coppice Farm. Amy turned her head away. Romantical nonsense was amazingly potent in its power to make fools of the wise.

# = 8 =

THREE WEEKS LATER, Amy stood in the lush drawing room of 12 New Street, Chelsea, with very cold feet despite it being a warm day in May. She was fully embarked on fortune hunting, and she *had* to succeed. It was all so horribly expensive.

Even though she, Beryl, and Jassy had worked together on her fine new wardrobe, some items had had to be purchased, and the cost of material alone had amounted to a frightening sum. The coach fare for her and Aunt Lizzie, along with the charges for food and lodging along the way, had been another burden.

There would be more expenses in the future, for though their hostess—Lizzie's cousin, Nell Claybury—appeared delighted to have them visit for as long as they pleased, there would be tickets, vouchers, and vails.

"Come sit down, Miss de Lacy, please," said Mrs. Claybury cheerfully. "I know after traveling for days you feel you never want to sit again, but truly you will feel better for a cup of tea." The plump lady patted the seat beside her and Amy went to take it.

Aunt Lizzie's cousin Nell was a still-pretty woman in her fifties, and if Amy suspected her chestnut curls owed something to artifice, she had to admit that it was well enough done so that one could not be entirely sure. The lady also appeared to have an amiable temperament and a genuinely kind disposition. More than these, however, it was the shrewd common sense she detected in Nell Claybury that attracted Amy.

"You are a treat for the eyes, Miss de Lacy," the woman said frankly and turned to Aunt Lizzie. "I can quite see why you wanted to bring her to Town, Lizzie. She'll make a fine match, no doubt of it." She glanced at Amy. Heaven knows what she saw there. Amy thought that her expression must have hinted at her fears, for Mrs. Claybury quickly went on, "But no need to talk of such things just yet. So tired as you both must be. After tea you must go to your rooms and have a nice lie down. We'll have a quiet dinner, just the three us, and then you can have an early night. Tomorrow I'll show you some of the sights. You'll like that, my dear," she said kindly to Amy, as if Amy were a child. "We'll go to the ·Queen's Palace. You may catch sight of the queen, or one of the princesses."

Amy sipped the excellent tea and let the chatter wash over her as Nell told of her life alone here since her husband died some two years since. Her two sons, both occupied in the family ship chandlery, chose to keep their own establishments, and so this fine house, built ten years ago, was left just to her. Her two daughters were married and living away from London.

"So you can see how pleased I am to have company, and an excuse to gad about!"

Amy smiled. The pleasure was clearly genuine, and it lightened her burdens to think that this kind lady was going to benefit from the enterprise. All that remained was to be sure that Aunt Lizzie was correct in saying that Nell Claybury moved in the highest circles of the city. The house and its location was very promising.

New Street had been as recently built as its name suggested, and if one were set down here by magic, it would be hard to tell one was not in Mayfair; there was even a square, Hans Place, very close by. Instead of the most fashionable part of Town, however, this was an area of rich merchants. Many of the surrounding streets were of simpler houses, doubtless inhabited by the ambitious clerks who worked in the city.

Next day Amy thoroughly enjoyed the carriage tour of London, as if she truly were a child being given a treat, and she stored up all the details so that she could write of them to the family back home. And soon, if she was successful, her family would be here to delight in the sights themselves.

The sun was shining, and the city appeared at its best despite the noise and dirt. Trees were in bright leaf in the parks and squares, and flowers made brave splashes of color.

Everyone, even those in rags, seemed cheerful now that the Corsican Monster was safely tucked away on the island of Elba, and Bourbon cockades and fleurs-de-lis had sprouted with the spring flowers. In various places preparations were already under way for the grand victory celebrations which would mark the visit of the tsar of Russia and the king of Prussia.

The Claybury coachman took them past a host of fine buildings, new and old. The Houses of Parliament, the Royal Exchange, and Westminster Hall had graced London for centuries; Somerset House, the Royal Circus, and the Lord Mayor's House were new additions. Mrs. Claybury promised Amy visits to many of these places in the weeks to come. Almack's Assembly Rooms were pointed out, and the homes of some of the famous—Holland House, Carlton House, and Devonshire House.

Amy thanked her warmly, for she could see the lady took genuine pleasure in pleasing others, but she couldn't help a pang of dismay. Here she was gawking like a yokel at places to which she was entitled entry by birth.

Had she come to London as Amy de Lacy of Stonycourt, the daughter of a rich baronet, rather than the poor guest of a merchant's widow, she might well have attended a ball at Holland House, and received vouchers for Almack's. It was more than likely that she would have attended an event at Carlton House.

But she firmly put such unworthy repinings behind her. She had set her course and would hold to it. Her family depended on her.

That very evening she was given the opportunity to begin. Their hostess had an invitation to an evening of cards and music to which she had been urged to bring her guests.

"Clara Trueblood always does things very well," said Mrs. Claybury. "There'll be plenty of younger people for Amy, and," she added meaningfully, "some older, warmer ones, too."

Amy had insisted that their hostess know of her plans, but this plain speaking made her color.

"Don't you be missish, dear," said Nell comfortably. "Most young ladies are out to make a good marriage, and with your looks you'll have no trouble at all. There's a lot to be said for knowing what you plan to make when you start to bake. Not but what," she added thoughtfully, "you might do better to introduce yourself to some of your highborn connections and move in better circles. Looks like yours come once in a decade, dear."

Amy had regained her composure. "It would not serve, ma'am. It would be much more expensive to cut a dash in Mayfair. Even the rent of a house is beyond us. Besides that, many of the ton are land rich but not overendowed with cash to put into Stonycourt."

"You had best make sure any gentleman who courts you is willing to lay out his blunt, dear, or you could get a sad surprise, be he ever so rich."

"Oh, I know that," said Amy. "I intend to be completely honest about it when the time comes."

Nell nodded, but she still looked dubious. "Even if you are seeking a wealthy city man, it would do no harm for you to attend a few fashionable affairs. In fact, it would doubtless raise your value considerably."

Amy experienced a stab of alarm. Cutting a dash among the ton was no part of her plans. "I do hope not, ma'am, for I have no intention of moving in those circles. I doubt if I could anyway. Our connections are limited. My father had only one sister and she lives in Cumberland. I have cousins but I don't know if they are in Town. There are doubtless friends, both from school and from home, but not close enough for us to expect them to sponsor me." She smiled at Mrs. Claybury, for she had developed a genuine fondness for the lady. "Not everyone is as generous as you, ma'am."

The woman colored with pleasure. "Oh poo. I simply hate being here all on my own. The next few months are going to be the most delightful I've had in years. The whole of London will be in festival for the victories, and I will enjoy it a great deal more in young company. Besides," she added naughtily, "I can't wait to see all the gentlemen of my acquaintance make perfect nodcocks of themselves over you."

Amy joined her new friend in laughter and felt a good deal better about everything.

The Claybury party arrived at the Trueblood's rout fashionably late, and to Amy's eyes it appeared grand enough to be a ton affair. The hosts had hired rooms at the Swan, and by the time Amy and her party arrived, those rooms were pleasantly full of a hearty throng. The gentlemen were all fine; the ladies smart. There was no shortage of beautiful garments and costly jewels.

Tables were set up in one room and were being well used by card players. Amy was pleased to see, however, that there was none of the tense atmosphere she would expect from high gaming, and the coins in use were mainly pennies, thruppences, and sixpences. It didn't appear anyone was likely to lose their all here.

Another room was arranged for rest and conversation and included lavish amounts of food and drink. A great many of the older people were settled there.

A third room was a ballroom, where a trio worked away in one corner, playing cheerful country dances. Despite her determination not to take pleasure in this mission, Amy's toe began to tap. It had been so long since she had attended a dance. She waited for some gentleman to ask her to dance and did not have to wait long.

Heads had turned as they passed through the rooms. People had stared. Amy had always attracted attention, even in the dull clothes she had chosen in the past. Dressed as she was now in a pale pink silk gown with bodice of deep pink satin trimmed with beads, she knew she was unignorable. Especially, she admitted ruefully, as the bodice was fashionably low. It had been Beryl who had insisted on that, and Amy rather wished she hadn't given in. She felt horribly exposed.

But that, or her other endowments, attracted the young men like a blossom attracts bees. They gathered, they hovered. Amy wondered which would prove boldest.

It was a bright-eyed and dashing young man called Charles Nolan. He had fashionable windswept dark hair and too many showy fobs.

"He who hesitates is lost," he quoted cheerfully as he led her into the set.

Amy smiled at him. "Are you usually so quick to act, sir?"

"Of course. I find it serves me well. I am fast making my fortune by means of seeing opportunities and taking them."

He clearly intended this to be a point in his favor, but Amy immediately crossed him off her list of possibilities. Up and coming hopefuls were of no use to her. She had never expected to find her fortune attached to a young man anyway.

Mr. Nolan was succeeded by Mr. Hayport; Mr. Hayport by Mr. Jackson. She was careful to appear amiably feather-headed, for she had settled on that role. Her appearance seemed to lead people to leap to that conclusion anyway, and so she would allow it as gentlemen appeared to be much happier without a challenge to their own intellects.

None of her partners were eligible but Amy enjoyed herself tremendously. Then her conscience began to prick.

This would not do at all. She would never meet the older, richer men while prancing on the dance floor. When the next partner presented, she pleaded exhaustion and asked him to take her to the refreshment room.

He collected wine for them and sat beside her. This

gentleman was Peter Cranfield. He was a little older than her previous partners and of a more serious disposition. He did not seem at all put out to be spending his time with her in conversation rather than dancing.

He tactfully made it clear that he came of a very wealthy family, but he also told Amy that he was one of three sons who would inherit the business and their father was still hale and hearty. Amy felt rather sorry for him, for he clearly thought himself a very fine fellow. She hoped this prime article wouldn't precipitately propose.

Amy missed a great deal of Mr. Cranfield's subtle self-advertisement in a fruitless review of a certain disastrous encounter. Even though the result could never have been different, she had wished and wished again that her last moments with Harry Crisp had not been so horrible.

"Well, Peter, you have carried off the prize. I admire such enterprise."

Amy looked up quickly to see an older man by their table. He was a trim man with silver hair, fine bones, and heavy-lidded gray eyes.

Mr. Cranfield rose, rather reluctantly. "Thank you, Uncle. Miss de Lacy, may I make known to you my uncle, Sir Cedric Forbes?" Amy acknowledged the introduction. "And this, Uncle, is Miss Amy de Lacy of Lincolnshire. She is a guest of Mrs. Claybury."

Sir Cedric sat at the table. Despite his age—for he must have been in his fifties—he was still a handsome man and had an air of intelligence and authority.

He immediately took over the steering of the conversation. Not a mention of money now, but talk of the Frost Fair in February and the great snows which had followed; anticipation of the coming festivities and the political implications of peace. Amy enjoyed it tremendously, then began to fear she was appearing too intelligent.

"La," she said, with a flutter of her fan, "I cannot wait to see the tsar, Sir Cedric. He is said to be remarkably handsome."

Sir Cedric appeared amused but he also showed admiration. Amy's heart began to beat faster. Was this the one?

He was surely in control of his own fortune, but how great was it? There was nothing to tell from his appearance, which was elegant but unostentatious.

If he did prove suitable, she would be Lady Forbes, which would soothe her family.

"Handsome men are not that rare a sight, Miss de Lacy," he said in response to her inanity. "You will doubtless see many during your weeks in Town."

"Oh, I do hope so," fluttered Amy, feeling a perfect fool.

Sir Cedric turned to his nephew. "I am sure you have a partner awaiting you, Peter. I will take care of Miss de Lacy until she feels ready to dance again."

Mr. Cranfield took a disgruntled leave and Sir Cedric turned back to Amy. "Some more wine, Miss de Lacy?"

"That would be delightful, Sir Cedric."

As soon as it was provided, he considered her with appreciation and a glint of something which could be friendly, teasing, or flirtatious. "Do you concern yourself only with looks then, young lady?"

Trapped in her act of silliness, Amy almost blurted out that she also concerned herself about money. What would this man want to hear? At his age he doubtless took life very seriously. "Indeed no, Sir Cedric," she said, muting the simper a shade or two. "I do delight in a man of character and intelligence and I love to hear an erudite discussion."

"How unfortunate then," he said with a twinkle, "that the debating society at the Athenian Lyceum has ceased to meet. But we now have the Surrey Institution, where excellent lectures are given on a great many interesting subjects. If you would like, Miss de Lacy, I would be delighted to escort you and your aunt there one day soon. I know that Mrs. Claybury has little interest in such events."

Amy wasn't sure she did either but she expressed enthusiasm for the plan. He then discussed a bewildering range of intellectual diversions available in the capital until another young hopeful came to beg a dance.

Amy longed to be back on the floor but did not want to offend her potential Croesus.

"Please, Miss de Lacy," he said, "if you are rested, go and prance with this young fellow. I rarely dance anymore but I would not deny you the pleasure. I will make all the arrangements with your aunt for our visit to the Surrey Institution."

As she left the refreshment room, Amy felt as if she had acquired a tutor rather than a suitor, but having made such hopeful progress she abandoned herself to the joys of the dance until the early hours of the morning.

The three ladies were tired but content on the way home.

Aunt Lizzie had spent most of her time in the card room playing whist, a pleasure denied her since Sir Digby's death, since only Beryl and Amy could play a decent game, and Amy found little pleasure in it. Together with the enjoyment, she had the satisfaction of ending the evening six shillings the richer.

Nell Claybury had enjoyed her wide circle of friends. "And I declare," she said, "you danced every dance, Amy. You were a grand success. I expect my knocker to be constantly on the go now that you have been seen."

Though she knew it was true, Amy demurred. "Many of the callers will be for you, Mrs. Claybury. Whenever I looked around you were on the floor, too."

"I confess, I do love to dance," said Nell with a twinkle, "and there are usually some gentlemen gallant enough to take pity on an old lady."

Amy grinned at her. In her youthful pale green silk, Nell looked a good deal less than fifty. "I swear," Amy said, "I don't know how I am to catch a rich husband with you as competition."

"Flummery. And I doubt I have the mind to marry again. Did you meet anyone who interests you, dear?"

Amy was hesitant to put her hopes into words, but she

needed to know the extent of Sir Cedric's wealth and so she named him.

"My dear!" declared Nell. "He is a regular Midas. Or is that who I mean? Forbes Bank, you know."

Amy didn't, but a bank sounded just what she needed.

"Of course he is rather old," said Nell, "but still very handsome and so charming. He and my husband were good friends, but I haven't seen much of him these past few years."

"Is he a knight or a baronet?" asked Aunt Lizzie.

"Just a knight. For services to the realm," Nell said, then winked. "Something to do with Prinny's debts."

Aunt Lizzie wrinkled her nose but said, "Still, it will not be intolerable to have you Lady Forbes, Amethyst. It will sound quite well at home. He spoke to me about an entertainment he plans. He did seem to be a man of sense and elegance. No doubt he will do."

"Let us not go too fast," protested Amy. "His interest may be no more than avuncular."

Nell Claybury chuckled. "I doubt any man's interest in you is merely avuncular, Miss de Lacy. I declare the temperature in those rooms rose five degrees as you passed. You must live an interesting life."

Looking out the carriage window at the dark streets, Amy made no reply. She did not find her life interesting. Now that the excitement of the evening was behind her, and a victim was singled out, she realized her life was intolerably bleak.

"Wednesday night is Almack's night,"Chart chortled as he entered the handsome rooms he and Harry had taken in Chapel Street. With a man and wife to take care of domestic matters and Quincy and Gerrard to turn the young men out smart, they were very comfortable indeed. Or would be, he reflected, if Harry were his normal, lighthearted self.

Certainly Harry was acting the part tolerably well. He laughed at jokes and even told one now and then. He took interest in games of chance, pugilistic exploits, and salacious gossip. But there was a bitter edge to him that Chart had never seen before, and he was drinking too much.

Damn Amethyst de Lacy.

"Oh God," groaned Harry from where he sat slumped in a chair, cradling a glass of claret. "There'll be more than enough Wednesdays in the Season. I can't face it tonight."

"There are not that many Wednesdays in a Season," countered Chart firmly, "and when I talked my mother into getting us vouchers, I promised we'd be there tonight in case Clyta needs a partner."

Harry sighed and pushed up out of his chair. "Oh well, if it's for the lovely Clytemnestra."

"And for you," said Chart. "The sooner you settle on a bride the better."

"I've been doing the pretty at receptions and soirées for weeks, haven't I? Nothing but frightened sparrows and brazen hussies."

Chart restrained the urge to plant him a facer and knock some sense into him. "And which of those is my sister?"

Harry smiled, and looked for a moment like his old self. "Either a frightened hussy or a brazen sparrow. Has she decided quite what style she wants to develop?"

"No," said Chart with a sigh. "She's bold one moment and stammers the next. I hold it's the mixed influence of my eldest sister Cassandra, who has herself wrapped up so tight I'm surprised she can walk, and a lingering adoration of my scandalous sister, Chloe. At least with you there and Randal—for he's promised to attend—she won't be a wallflower."

"She won't anyway," said Harry. "She's a handsome specimen. Tell you what, Chart. Why don't I offer for Clyta? Solve all our problems."

"Over my dead body." Chart was as startled by his own words as Harry was.

The two friends looked at each other.

"May I ask why?" Harry asked coolly.

"Gads, I'm sorry," Chart said. "I didn't mean it like that. If you develop a fondness for her, nothing would please me more. But," he added firmly, "I don't want Clyta in a marriage of convenience. I'm sure they turn out damned inconvenient in the end."

# === 9 ===

HARRY DANCED WITH Clytemnestra Ashby twice and tried to induce by force a feeling of connubial warmth. It would be wonderfully convenient, but it didn't work.

She was a shapely young woman of average height and was blessed by a mass of dark curls, very fine blue eyes, and an excellent figure that could almost be called lush. She had looked womanly since she was fourteen, and now, with a coating of bronze, she could pass for a matron, which, in Harry's opinion was unfortunate. Inside this glittering shell she was clearly still the young, rather gauche girl he had so often encountered at Chart's home.

Her behavior, as predicted, wavered between over-fulfilling the promise of her appearance or lapsing into a hot-cheeked awkwardness more suited to a school-room. Harry could understand Chart's protective concern. It would be easy for a man to get the wrong idea about Clytemnestra Ashby.

Harry felt the same concern, but it was all brotherly. He could not imagine taking Clyta to wife.

As he held hands with her and danced down the line, he remembered how hard it had been to pretend to merely brotherly fondness with Amy de Lacy, the excitement he had felt at merely being in the same room as her. Would he ever feel that way about anyone else? Then he cursed himself for this weakness.

"What?" asked Clyta, missing a step. Her eyes were wide with alarm. "Did I do something wrong?"

110

He'd sworn aloud. "No, of course not," Harry said with a reassuring smile. "I . . . er . . . I just remembered something I've forgotten to do."

She looked at him dubiously as they settled to their places at the end of the line.

"Truly," he said across the gap.

She was reassured and smiled as they stepped together and joined hands. It turned into something twistedly seductive. "Not very flattering," drawled Clyta with a sultry look worthy of the demimonde. "Your thoughts should all be of me, sir."

Harry suppressed a groan. "Do stop that, Clyta. Just be yourself."

She flushed again. "But I am." They danced around each other. As they separated, she added anxiously, "I think."

Harry gave thanks he didn't have to steer Clyta through her first Season.

Other than Chart's sister, Harry followed his usual policy and worked his way methodically through the most eligible young women. He was determined to meet as many as possible so as to give himself the greatest chance of encountering a tolerable one. Amy de Lacy couldn't be the only charmer capable of stirring his blood. He had no fixed criteria and tried whatever presented—pretty or plain, witty or shy, tall or short. But he tried the rich ones first. Might as well marry a fortune as not.

There was not a one he felt any desire to share his life with. When he danced with the pretty Miss Frogmorton, who was quite an heiress to boot, he found himself wondering what this pattern card of perfection would do if caught in a deluge. It was impossible to imagine.

And why the hell was Amy de Lacy fixed in his mind like a family ghost?

It was all so depressing that when Randal's wife boldly asked him for a dance, he agreed.

"Are you so short of partners, Sophie?" he asked.

"Not at all," she replied. "I merely thought you deserved one dance of pleasure."

"And what is that supposed to mean?" he demanded.

She gave him a saucy look. "You know perfectly well. If you want my advice—and you don't, of course—you'll stop looking so hard."

"If I just ignore the problem, my future bride will appear one day like a genie from a bottle?"

Sophie laughed. "What a lovely thought!"

He couldn't help but laugh with her. It *was* a great relief to be with someone simply for the pleasure of it. "For some reason I doubt that a bride from a bottle would be suited to life at Hey Park."

This time he could dance without ulterior motives, and by the time the set was over he was feeling relaxed and more like himself than he had in weeks. As they strolled over to join Randal, Sophie asked, "What of Amy de Lacy? Do you still think of her?"

It was like a dash of icy water. "No," Harry said sharply. "Why would I?"

"Merely to rejoice in such a lucky escape," said Sophie lightly. "After all, I doubt there's a lady in this room who would reject your suit, never mind slap you for it."

Harry handed her over to her husband and stalked off without a word.

Randal looked down at his wife and raised a brow. "Distinctly frosty," he said. "Why do I have the feeling you've been meddling again, minx?"

She dimpled. "Because you know me so well? Harry's never going make a good choice of bride until he clears Amy de Lacy from his head."

"And you intend to help him with his spring cleaning? Sophie, from whence do you get this lamentable tendency to interfere?"

"I don't know," she said unrepentantly. "But I'm very good at it. Did I or did I not bring about the happy union of Ver and Emily?"

"I think they would have managed well enough on their own."

"Ha! There speaks the man who would have let me marry Trenholme out of a misguided sense of nobility."

He laughed. "Perhaps. I would probably have snatched you away at the altar like Lochinvar."

"Would you?" asked Sophie, much taken. "Then I wish I had accepted him."

He shook his head. "You're incorrigible. But at least in this case there's little mischief you can do, with Harry here and Amy de Lacy in Lincolnshire."

"No?" queried Sophie sweetly. "But this very morning I received a letter from Emily. They are on their way to Hampshire, but apparently as they left, gossip said that the beautiful Miss de Lacy has come to London for the Season. We could meet her anywhere." With a naughty grin at her alarmed husband, she swept off on the arm of another partner.

Amy and Aunt Lizzie were escorted by Sir Cedric to the lecture at the Surrey Institution. It proved to be on the plants of the Amazon. It was stupefyingly boring but afterward Amy eagerly accepted an invitation to attend another one the next week on the principles of steam locomotion. Sir Cedric was clearly interested in her, and he was exactly what she had come to London to find. She was not surprised, however, when Aunt Lizzie declined the treat, saying Amy hardly needed a chaperon to such an event.

Her aunt was pleased enough in the meantime to accompany Amy and her admirer to the Royal Academy, and to the British Museum to see the Egyptian antiquities. In her visions of a London Season, Amy had never imagined it to be quite so *educational*.

Each evening, however, there was a soirée, a rout, or an assembly to attend and ample opportunity to dance. Amy received three proposals in the first week, but, though at least one was unexceptionable, none of the gentlemen was rich enough for her purpose. At least, she thought wryly, she had learned to be a little more gracious in her refusals.

All her hopes lay with Sir Cedric.

Their second trip to the Surrey Institution was the first

time they had been out alone, and Amy was excited and yet nervous. If Sir Cedric suddenly became loverlike, what should she do?

"And are you enjoying your time in London, Miss de Lacy?"

"Very much, Sir Cedric. Everyone is most kind."

"I must confess that I am a little surprised that you are not moving in the higher reaches of society to which you are entitled."

Amy flicked a glance at him. Was he suspicious? She made a decision. "We can't afford it," she said bluntly.

He nodded slightly as if she had confirmed something he already knew. "But you would have no objection to attending fashionable events?"

"No," she said. "I have no family or close friends to sponsor me, however."

"If you accompany me, you would need no sponsor." He smiled at her unguarded look of amazement. "The barriers of Society are flexible, Miss de Lacy, particularly before the pressure of wealth. I receive a great many invitations and attend what functions please me. I would like to see you shine in your appropriate setting."

"I do not consider myself above my present company, sir."

"And I admire you for it. But you are above it, Miss de Lacy. You could have all London at your feet."

Amy was torn between a natural desire to enjoy the social pleasures she had been raised to expect, and a feeling that it would be most unwise. "Why do you wish to do this for me?" she asked.

He smiled slightly, almost ruefully. "I think it important, that is all. I have already received an invitation to Carlton House, to the fête for the victorious allies in July. If you are still in Town at the time I would like you to accompany me. And your aunt, of course."

Amy felt a tremor of nervous anticipation. This must presage an offer, and yet that question mark—"if you are still in Town"—made it uncertain. Did he need encouragement?

He did not seem to be at all unsure of himself as he continued, "And the Russian Embassy is to hold a reception in two weeks. Will you accompany me to it, Miss de Lacy? The haute ton will be there in force, and you did say you wished to see the tsar."

It was no part of Amy's plan to mix with the fashionable elite, but she suppressed her qualms. "I would be pleased to attend," she said firmly.

This second lecture proved to be a little more interesting than the first, as there were a number of models which hissed and turned under the influence of steam. The lecturer was concerned with the use of steam in industry and transportation. He claimed steam could one day replace horses, but Amy found it difficult to imagine a teakettle trundling up the North Road.

The steam made her think of kitchens, though. How useful it would be if steam could turn a spit, or power a dolly-stick to pummel a load of washing. She remembered Meg Coneybear and her energy, and the amount of work she would have on her hands all her life.

Harry Crisp would be interested in things like this, she thought, remembering the automaton. She wondered if he ever designed machines.

The lecturer was detailing some physical principle, which Amy found boring. She took to studying the assortment of people packing the lecture hall.

She and Sir Cedric were sitting at the front of the first gallery. Below them, on the floor of the hall were nine rows of banked seats, giving everyone an excellent view of the stage. Her eyes wandered the audience, which included all types of people, from the *ton* to threadbare students, scribbling notes.

It was because she had been thinking about Harry Crisp that one man looked like him.

Very like him.

The same crisp, tawny curls. Straight, broad shoulders . . .

A tingling chill passed through her. It couldn't be. It had to be her imagination. The gentleman was in the third row in the hall. She could really only see the back of his head and one ear.

But it was Harry Crisp. She knew it, and felt this urgent desire to leap to her feet and flee.

It was impossible, seated as they were in the middle of a row. Anyway, nothing would serve better to draw attention to her, especially as the lecturer had paused to set up his next demonstration. People were conversing with their neighbors and glancing around. Amy wished she could slide down and hide.

Harry turned to speak to a pretty young lady by his side, smiling at her words. Amy felt her teeth clench together at the sight.

Sir Cedric asked how she was enjoying the lecture. Amy turned to him with a brilliant smile and assured him she was fascinated. Harry Crisp was nothing to her, nothing.

But as the lecture resumed, her eyes were drawn back to him and his party. The young woman leaned to her other side to make a quiet comment to a handsome blond man. Perhaps he was her partner, not Harry. On Harry's other side was a gray-haired man. Amy ignored the speaker and studied the trio for any further sign of their alignment.

Did people really feel eyes upon them? The blond man turned. His eyes locked with Amy's and he stared at her. He was truly the most handsome she had ever seen and she found she could not look away. Amy feared she was going mad. Then his lips curved in a thoughtful, intrigued smile before he turned away.

Short of breath, Amy concentrated her gaze on the stage and planned how she could get herself and Sir Cedric out of the building ahead of the crowd.

They were seated not very far from the stairs, but Sir Cedric had, on the last visit, showed a habit of waiting for the crush to abate before leaving. That would be disastrous, for she would be fixed here like an object on display as the people filing out of the lower hall passed within feet of her. Instead they must be first out.

As soon as the lecture was over, she put her hand to her head. "Oh, Sir Cedric. I feel faint. Please, let us leave quickly!"

He was all concern. "My dear Miss de Lacy. You should have spoken before. It will be far better now to wait a few minutes rather than leave in this crush." He used his program to fan her vigorously.

The moment had been lost and the stairs were already filling. She could see Harry Crisp and his friends already on their feet. They would turn at any moment. The blond man did turn his head slightly and raised his brows to see her sitting there.

She leapt to her feet. "I will feel better if I am moving," she declared. "Please let us go."

"Very well," said a worried Sir Cedric. "Come along." He put his hand on her elbow and steered her toward the stairs. Once there, however, the pressure of his hand turned her down them, not up.

"What are you doing?" Amy cried.

"You are not well, Miss de Lacy. There is an exit behind the stage. I am sure we will be able to use it."

Amy pulled out of his grasp. "I am already much recovered," she insisted and turned to join the line leaving the hall.

But the damage had been done. Harry Crisp had seen her. He went pale and almost looked as if he would speak, though there would be no point at such a distance unless he were to bellow. Then he turned his attention back to his companions.

It was not a cut. At such a distance there was no question of such a thing. But it felt like one to Amy. It felt like a sword in the heart. Seeing him again, she realized her feelings went far deeper than she had ever thought possible after such brief acquaintance.

If only, if only, her father had not been so foolishly improvident, how happy she could have been.

In the carriage, Randal opened the subject with ruthless good humor. "That, I suppose, was Amethyst de Lacy."

Harry was staring out of the window. His head jerked around. "Why do you suppose such a thing?"

"I was told she was a diamond of the first water, and they don't come any more beautiful than that. Or at least, she's the only raving beauty I can imagine staring at you in such a way."

"Staring?"

"Assuredly."

"Damn impudence!" snapped Harry, then colored. "Sorry, Sophie."

"Not at all," she said amiably. "Was I the only one attending to the lecture?"

"I was attending," said Harry, and proved it by grimly discussing steam engines all the way to Mayfair.

When Randal dropped him off in Chapel Street, however, Harry asked as if impelled, "Who was that old man she was with? A relative, I suppose."

"Quite possibly," said Randal. "I think it was Sir Cedric Forbes, the banker." His mouth turned up in a wicked smile. "Doubtless a very high bidder."

Harry slammed the door of the coach.

As the coach rolled off, Sophie said, "Was that not a little unkind?"

" 'Tis cruel to be kind," Randal mused, absentmindedly drawing his wife into his arms. "I think your instinct is once more correct. It is time to meddle."

"But if she was with a rich, old banker she really is a fortune hunter. Harry is well rid of her."

"But does he know that? And she may have declared herself a fortune hunter, but the girl I saw back there was looking at Harry as if he were a lost treasure." He looked down at Sophie and smiled. "As if he were something very precious which she could not have. I know that feeling."

Sophie colored. "You only ever had to ask."

"It didn't seem that way at the time."

"You think this, too, may be a misunderstanding?"

"I don't know, but like all happily married people, I want to propel my friends into the same state. I do not see either Harry or the exquisite Miss de Lacy heading that way, and I think it behooves us to try to steer them aright."

Chart was summoned to Upper Brook Street. To Randal and Sophie's surprise he brought his sister Clyta with him.

"She has an important contribution to make," he announced.

Clyta looked flustered but said, "Amy de Lacy was a school friend. She was always kind to me. I'd like to help her if I can."

"Well," said Randal, "we're not at all sure the objects of our concern will appreciate our meddling, but you could certainly play a strong part in our plans."

"What are our plans?" asked Chart.

It was Sophie who outlined them. "Amy de Lacy and Harry only really met a few times. There was the storm, the tea party, and a few moments in the garden." She wrinkled her brow. "It almost defies belief that they could have got in such a muddle over tea."

"Really?" queried Randal with a heavy-lidded smile. "I remember a tea party at Maria Harroving's and some cakes . . ."

"Yes well," said Sophie, turning rosy. "But that was hardly the first time we'd met."

"Nor was tea the first time Harry met his fatal charmer."

"No, that was the storm," said Chart, "and we don't know what happened there."

"What we do know," said Sophie, taking control again, "is that neither of them was unaffected. Two meetings later he asked her to marry him and she hit him. Neither action indicates indifference. Clyta, does it surprise you to hear that Amy hit him?"

"Yes," said Clyta, eyes very wide. "Amy is gentle and sweet. She doesn't give in to unkind impulses."

Sophie nodded and continued. "Harry acts like a scalded cat if ever the woman's name is mentioned, and if Randal is correct, she was looking at Harry with her heart in her eyes." She frowned at her husband. "It doesn't make sense when she rejected him."

"And dash it all," said Chart, "they only met three times, and two of them were so brief as to be of no account!"

"So who believes in love at first sight?" mused Randal. "The point is, be it love or infatuation, it is a case of absence making the heart grow fonder. We must bring them together so they can either work out their differences or work out their obsession. Moving as they do in different circles, this will not be easy."

Sophie said, "A little investigation has revealed that she is staying with a Mrs. Claybury in Chelsea. A ship chandler's widow. A wealthy lady but not one who moves among the ton. That doesn't make sense either," she said with a sigh. "This is all a conundrum. I can't wait until it is solved." She looked, bright eyed, at her husband. "Shall we invade the cits, Randal, Harry in tow?"

"I fear he'd have to be in chains," Randal replied.

Clyta spoke up. "Why don't I simply invite her to my ball next week? I'm sure she'd like to come."

Everyone smiled. "Perfect, and perfectly simple," said Randal. "Congratulations, Clyta. But deliver the invitation in person, cousin. She may take a little persuading now she knows Harry is in Town."


When Clytemnestra Ashby called, Amy began to feel she was assaulted on all sides.

After the encounter, if such it could be called, with Harry Crisp at the Surrey Institution she had revoked her acceptance of Sir Cedric's invitations to the Russian Embassy and to Carlton House. She could not, would not, move in circles where she might encounter Harry Crisp face to face.

Sir Cedric, however, was proving to be unfortunately persistent and had recruited Aunt Lizzie and Nell Claybury to his side. Amy had no idea what he thought to gain from it, for Aunt Lizzie clearly supported Amy's move into higher circles in the hope that she would find a better match.

"I have always said it," Lizzie declared as they retrimmed Amy's pink dress with blond lace. "You have only to be seen."

"But there's no point to it," Amy protested. "Sir Cedric is clearly very interested in me. I don't need any other suitors."

"If you're set on him," said Lizzie tartly, jabbing a needle through the lace, "then you'd be best advised to conform to his wishes."

"We are going to the theater tomorrow," Amy pointed out. "That is at his insistence. And if the haute ton are going to swoon at my feet, that will give them ample opportunity."

"That is not the same thing," said Aunt Lizzie, stopping work and looking up. "Think how it would have pleased your dear mother to see you take your proper place."

Amy reflected that there was no weapon too low for Aunt Lizzie. "I will flaunt myself before the ton with pleasure, Aunt, when I am married." She abandoned her work to go and stare out the window.

Nell Claybury entered to catch the last of this.

"It is perfectly understandable, Amy, that Sir Cedric wishes to be seen with you among the fashionable throng. Any man would be proud to have you on his arm, and your gentle birth merely increases the effect."

"And if I do not care to be shown off like Napoleon's Eagles—a prize of war?"

Nell sat to take up Amy's work. "You were admirably honest, my dear, about your purpose in coming here. You should not cavil now."

Amy could feel her face heat. "I am not caviling. He can crow over his victory all he wishes within his own circle."

"But the ton is his circle, too. The walls dividing Society are less high and strong than you seem to imagine. It is almost," Nell added thoughtfully, "as if you are avoiding something. Is there perhaps a scandal attached to your name?"

Amy swallowed. "No. Except, of course, my father losing his money. But there are no unpaid creditors."

Nell looked up. "Then I cannot see how a little mingling with the glittering elite can harm you, Amy, and it seems important to the man you seek to win."

Amy failed to find a response and took refuge in her room.

It was ridiculous, perhaps, to fear the meeting so much. Among the hordes of people gathered for the Season, there was no reason she should encounter Harry Crisp at all. If she did, it would only be a momentary embarrassment. He would surely be as eager to avoid her as she was to avoid him.

Amy shivered. It wasn't that simple. She realized she was twirling something around her finger and looked down. Unconsciously she had opened a drawer and taken out this tuft of wool, the one he had gathered for her from a hedge an eon ago.

This wasn't the first time she had handled it like this, and it was now soiled and twisted into a crude kind of yarn. Impatiently she moved to throw it on the fire, but of course there was no fire in the grate in this warm weather. As she looked for a place to destroy the foolish memento, there was a scratch on the door.

Amy shoved the wool back in the drawer. "Yes?"

A maid entered and presented a card. "There's a young lady calling, miss."

Amy looked. "Good heavens. Clyta! I will be down in a minute."

She found her guest being entertained by Nell in the best reception room, tea already ordered by her kind hostess. As soon as Amy appeared, Mrs. Claybury excused herself.

"Clyta," Amy declared with delight. "Goodness, it must be quite two years since we parted at the doors to Miss Mallory's."

"And promised to write every day," said Clyta, hugging her friend. "I did write. I am sure it was you who stopped, you know."

"You are probably correct," Amy admitted ruefully. Even the cost of a letter had been a consideration, and time to write had been scarce. "Things have been difficult, I'm afraid." She was determined to get her dirty laundry out in the open immediately. But the thought flashed a memory of wringing a blue dress dry and ending up so close to Harry Crisp. Oh, she hated the way her mind played these tricks.

"What do you mean?" prompted Clyta, and Amy realized she had lapsed into silence.

"My father died soon after I left school. We found we were all rolled up."

"Oh," said Clyta. "I'm sorry."

Amy shrugged. "We've managed. But I'm afraid I found I had very little time." She smiled at her friend. "I am delighted to see you again, though. How on earth did you find me?"

"It is a little out of the way," said Clyta, then colored at what could be seen as snobbery. "I . . . er . . . saw you drive by and made inquiries. I simply had to come and call."

It sounded a little strange, but Amy did not feel she could question the story. "So you are doing the Season," she said. "I thought you would have made your curtsy last year."

Clyta blushed. "No. Mama delayed, hoping I would gain more composure, as she puts it. I think now she's decided that rather than becoming more composed, I'm decomposing due to old age. So here I am."

Amy gave Clyta's hand a comforting squeeze and wished she were in a position to help her. Clyta's problem had always been that she was painfully shy with strangers, and yet with her strong, mature looks she did not appear so. She had developed an excellent ability to act a part but not always the part appropriate to the moment.

"I'm sure you are a great success," she said.

"I don't know," said Clyta sadly. "I'm not ambitious. All I want, Amy, is to find a man I can be comfortable with. Someone who'll treat me like Chart or H— Oh well," she said gaily. "One day I'll meet my hero. But Amy, dearest, it would be so easier if I had your company."

Amy stared and tried to understand this sudden change. For a little while Clyta had been herself; now she was acting the part of the gay Society miss. That probably meant she was unhappy about something.

Amy tried a light tone. "I don't see how it would help to have me acting your shadow."

Clyta giggled. "Well, for one thing, it would attract all the men like honey." Amy let the silence run while Clyta fiddled with her reticule. In the end Clyta said, "It's just that I usually feel like being myself when I'm with you, Amy. I don't know why. I think it's because you're always honest with yourself."

"Am I?" asked Amy, guiltily aware that she'd been acting a part for weeks.

"Yes," said Clyta firmly. "You don't watch people, trying to guess what they want and then trying to be it. It's horrible actually, but I can't seem to help it."

Yes, it is horrible, thought Amy. She took her friend's hand again. "Oh, Clyta, what is it you want of me?"

Clyta gripped Amy's hand. "Will you come to my ball next week?" she said in a rush. "It will be fun if you're there. We can ask your aunt and Mrs. Claybury. I'm sure they'd like it, too. Please say yes. I need you, Amy. And that," she added, with strange intensity, "is the truth."

Amy stared at Clyta. It looked like a conspiracy, but that was ridiculous. There was no connection between Sir Cedric and the Ashbys. "I was not intending to move in such high circles," she demurred.

"Why not?" asked Clyta. "You're entitled to. I'm sure there will be any number of people there you know."

That was what Amy was afraid of. She wanted to ask if Clyta knew Harry Crisp but didn't dare. Then she realized something. "Good Lord. Your brother's Chart, isn't he?"

Clyta nodded, looking scared.

"You only ever used to call him Charteris."

Clyta licked her lips. "That's because Mama insisted. But he prefers to be called Chart. Do you know him?"

"We met once," said Amy dryly. "I suppose he is in Town."

Clyta nodded, and the guilt was clear on her face.

Amy knew then if she went to Clyta's ball she would at least be in the same room as Harry Crisp. Chart Ashby would bring his friend along, and there might be some plan afoot to bring them face to face, though why Amy could not imagine. Were they planning revenge by humiliating her in public? She remembered her shift, but surely they wouldn't sink so low as to shame her at Clyta's ball.

And Clyta probably did need her support. It had never been easy for her to make friends. Amy couldn't imagine that Clyta would be part of a malicious plot against her.

Amy thought of Clyta's belief that she was so honest. Perhaps the time had come for honesty. It was ridiculous to be pretending to be a pretty wigeon in order to catch a husband. She couldn't keep it up for the rest of her life. It was equally silly to be hiding for fear of meeting a gentleman she hardly knew.

She would be herself, face down the devil, and by showing that she belonged in the very highest stratas of Society, bring Sir Cedric to the point.

"I will be delighted to attend, Clyta," said Amy.

# =10=

CHART WAS CONVINCED his hair was turning gray by the minute. It was close to the time to leave for his sister's ball, and Harry was sitting in his shirtsleeves playing with a doll. The music tinkled and the dancing lady raised her leg and pointed her toe.

"Will you stop fiddling with that damned thing!" he snapped.

Harry looked up with an ironic smile. "Why the heat? Clyta doesn't care whether I attend or not." There was a *ping*, and the dancer's leg went limp.

"Yes she does. She asked after you particularly."

Harry looked up from the mechanism to raise an unusually cynical brow. "If she's developed a crush on me, I'd best stay away. You were right. We wouldn't suit."

Chart walked over, picked up the automaton, and placed it on the sideboard. "She does not have a crush on you, but she's nervous and wants a horde of handsome young men to do her proud, at least some of them not related. You're coming."

Harry gave a brief laugh and rose. "If it means that much." He went to a mirror and inspected his cravat, rearranging the folds slightly. "I suppose Lucy Frogmorton may be there. I suspect I may end up married to her."

Chart could feel more gray hairs sprouting by the minute.

Clyta's ball was to be held at the magnificent mansion belonging to her uncle, the Duke of Tyne. As the Claybury carriage set them down in front of it, Amy reflected that she might have been hasty in writing off the fortunes of the ton. Some people were obviously still very rich.

"It is a very fine house, isn't it?" said Sir Cedric as he assisted her down. It had turned out that he, too, had an invitation to this event and so he had arranged to escort them. On the whole, Amy was pleased. She would be able to show him she wasn't afraid of moving in high circles, and—should the worst happen—he would form a buffer between herself and Harry Crisp.

Amy kept to her resolution and ceased acting a part. She did not know whether Sir Cedric noticed it or not, but it had certainly not diluted his regard. Amy had no doubt he felt warmly toward her and she waited anxiously for him to address the subject of marriage. The sooner it was settled, the sooner she could go home.

"It is magnificent," she replied. "And with all the windows lit it looks like a fairy palace." Feeling bold, she added. "What is your house like, Sir Cedric?"

"Not nearly so fine as this, I'm afraid, but I think it a pleasant home. Perhaps tomorrow you and your aunt would take tea there."

There, thought Amy with a glow of triumph, that wasn't so hard. "I must ask Aunt Lizzie, but I do not believe we have any engagements."

In fact, as they worked their way up the stairs, she began to think that she might be able to prompt Sir Cedric to speak of marriage tonight. She knew she looked her best, and the startled attention she was garnering from every quarter confirmed it.

On hearing of the invitation, Nell Claybury had insisted on ordering a special dress for Amy, and no protest had been able to dissuade her. The kind woman was so cock-a-hoop to be going to a ball at a ducal mansion that she clearly needed to make some gesture in return. In the end Amy had given in.

They had decided to give the order to Mrs. Littlewood, Nell's normal dressmaker, rather than try a new and more fashionable one. The woman had easily risen to the challenge. They had all worked together to pick a design and adapt it, for, said Mrs. Littlewood shrewdly, looks like Amy's did not need ornamenting and simplicity would serve them better than flounces.

The gown was of cream satin under a tunic of white lace dusted with tiny golden beads. It fell smooth without flounce or fringing. On the very short bodice the beads were arranged in a pattern of leaves, and the same design decorated the puffed sleeves. Golden ribbons were woven through Amy's curls, and around her neck she wore a pretty, delicate golden necklace set with pearls, which Nell Claybury had lent her.

Though she had set out to look her best, as the gasps and whispers marked her progress, Amy began to feel her usual embarrassment.

Nell Claybury leaned forward and murmured. "Goodness, it's just like being in a play, isn't it, dear?"

Amy looked around and decided it was. Everyone was posing and preening, and delivering witty lines which often sounded rehearsed. Her part, it would appear, was fairy princess. So be it. She flashed a grateful smile at Nell, raised her chin, and prepared to enjoy herself.

In the receiving line, Clyta's parents were haughty but pleased to approve of "one of the Lincolnshire de Lacys." Clyta was handsome in pale blue lace and bubbling with excitement and nervousness, which was a dangerous combination. "Just be yourself, dear," Amy whispered before she had to move on.

To Chart Ashby.

He took her hand. "Miss de Lacy."

"Mr. Ashby." Amy tried to read his face and couldn't. He was acting as if they were slight acquaintances. That was true, of course, but was that all? She had the sudden paralyzing image of Harry Crisp saying, "Who? Amy de Lacy? Oh yes. Met her in the Shires somewhere."

She found herself well advanced into the room with no idea how she had come there.

"You are looking faint again, Miss de Lacy," said Sir Cedric with concern. "I do not think crowds agree with you."

Amy plied her ivory fan. "You may be correct. Perhaps we could move closer to the windows."

Harry watched Amy numbly.

A hum in the room had alerted him. It was nothing definite, just a change in the tone of the voices all around. It drew his attention and focused it—focused it on a vision in white and gold floating through the glittering throng and making everyone else look decidedly shabby.

Amethyst de Lacy, smiling, at ease, and looking like a princess.

What a fool he'd been to even imagine she would marry him. She was fit for a king, or at least a duke. He glanced sideways at the Duke of Rowanford—young and eligible.

"Who in God's name is that?" asked Rowanford in a reverent whisper.

"Amethyst de Lacy of Lincolnshire," said Harry coolly.

Rowanford looked at him. "You know her, Harry? Care to introduce me?"

Harry almost laughed, but then he thought, Why not? and led the way over to Amy. She was with her aunt, another older woman, and that damned banker. He wondered cynically what she'd do when she had to choose between a young, wealthy duke and an older, much wealthier banker. This should be amusing.

She was facing away from him, so he had the advantage of surprise. "Miss de Lacy."

She turned quickly, pale, and with huge eyes. He remembered her looking like that in the kitchen at Coppice Farm before he'd set himself out to soothe her. What on earth was she afraid of now with friends, relatives, and the whole of Society at her back? Probably that he'd expose her for the greedy, heartless harpy she was.

"Mr. Crisp," she said faintly. He saw her swallow.

He indicated Rowanford. "Beg leave to present my friend, the Duke of Rowanford, Miss de Lacy." As she extended her hand he added, "Rowanford, Miss de Lacy."

He watched cynically as she chatted and promised the duke the supper dance. She was making no particular play to catch Rowanford's interest, but then she didn't need to. Her damn beauty did it all for her. She'd ensnared Harry dressed in a blanket, and now she had the finest gown a London modiste could provide.

What had happened to her poverty? he wondered cynically. She'd doubtless been borrowing against expectations.

Rowanford dug him in the ribs, "Wits wandering, Harry? You should grab a dance now before the hordes descend."

Harry looked to Amy for any indication of her feelings, but her face was as smooth as the porcelain features of Lady Jane. As well be hung for a sheep as a lamb. "May I have the first waltz, Miss de Lacy?"

Her eye widened, and he only then realized she could hardly say no. "Of course, Mr. Crisp."

He looked so strange, thought Amy. Pale, not the least like smiling. But he had come over to her. No one had forced him. And why on earth had he asked her for a dance, for a waltz?

She didn't know what it was going to be like to swirl round and round in his arms. She didn't want to think about it.

The music finally began for the first dance, and Sir Cedric led her out into the same set as Clyta, who was partnered by her brother. Sir Cedric rarely danced, but he had claimed "the first dance with the most beautiful woman in the room." Amy told herself that this warm flattery sounded very hopeful and smiled up at him. He was very handsome and distinguished and fit into this company perfectly. There would be no need to blush for her husband.

Then Harry joined them. His partner was the girl he'd been with at the Surrey Institution. She was pretty, elegant, and sparkled with vitality. She said something to Harry and he laughed with honest amusement.

Amy couldn't help it. She was assailed by searing, irrational jealousy. She had to know.

She moved a step closer to Clyta. "Who is the auburn-haired woman?"

Clyta had the tremulous blankness she always had when she was feeling nervous or guilty. "Oh her!" she said with piercing gaiety. "That's Sophie. Lady Randal Ashby. Randal's our cousin, isn't he, Chart?"

"Was last time I thought about it," said Chart dryly. "Calm down, Clyta."

Clyta calmed like a pricked bubble. Really, thought Amy as the music began, a Season could be cruel torment for someone like Clyta. She had the feeling her friend had been doing a little scheming and was nervous about it, but she could hardly task her with it when Clyta was already in a state.

Besides, she and Harry had met and the world had not ended, and Harry was dancing with a safely married lady.

It was only as she curtsied to Sir Cedric that she saw him glance thoughtfully at Harry Crisp. She set out to charm his mind away from the subject.

Amy's next partner was the Duke of Rowanford, who had turned greedy and demanded another dance before the supper one. She smiled to think how delighted Aunt Lizzie would be to see her dance twice with a duke. He was even that rare specimen, a young and handsome duke, with wavy brown hair and rather soulful dark eyes.

"You smile?" he asked. "Why?"

"Because I have finally met a duke," Amy said in her new spirit of honesty. "My family have always been of the opinion that I should marry a duke."

After a startled moment he laughed. When the dance brought them back together he said, "Are you not afraid of being thought bold, Miss de Lacy?"

"Why is that bold? I'll go odds half the women in this room think they should marry a duke."

He grinned. "I'd have to cut myself into tiny pieces. There aren't many of us available."

"That," she pointed out, "is why you are so sought after, your grace."

He laughed again. "You are set on deflating my pride, I see. Pray tell me, Miss de Lacy, where have you sprung from?"

"Chelsea," she said blithely as she danced off into a new pattern.

As they promenaded afterward he said, "Are you, like Cinderella, going to disappear at midnight, Miss de Lacy?"

"I hardly think so, your grace. But don't expect to see me again at these events. I only came to oblige Clyta Ashby. In fact, I think I should go and speak to her, if we could progress in that direction."

It was as they worked their way toward Clyta that Amy realized she had created great problems for herself this evening. She had promised to be with her friend, but that would throw her in with Chart Ashby, and doubtless Harry Crisp as well. Moreover, this would not allow much opportunity to work a declaration out of Sir Cedric. To make matters worse, the duke seemed inclined to attach himself to her, and Sir Cedric might gain the impression that she was throwing him over for bigger game.

It might, of course, stimulate jealousy, but Amy judged Sir Cedric as too cool and mature to allow himself to be manipulated by that base emotion.

When they arrived at the group which centered on Clyta, Amy saw that Harry's dancing partner, Sophie, was there along with the handsome blond man of the Surrey Institution. She was introduced to Clyta's cousin Lord Randal Ashby, son of the Duke of Tyne who owned this house.

Was it her imagination the Ashbys looked at her with particular attention?

As she tried to calm Clyta and bolster her confidence, Amy was most uncomfortable herself. These were Harry's friends and they must know of her wretched behavior. What did they think of her?

Where was he?

The music struck up for the first waltz and Harry appeared at her side, face guarded. "This is our dance, I believe, Miss de Lacy."

As she turned to go with him, she saw astonishment of varying degrees on the faces around.

"I am sure there is no need for this dance, sir," she said coolly as he led her onto the floor. "I am quite willing to pretend some sort of indisposition."

His face was a mask of courtesy. "I asked you to partner me and you accepted. There is no need to fuss."

"I could hardly refuse without seeming intolerably rude."

"I would not have thought such considerations would bear heavily upon you, Miss de Lacy."

Amy gasped and would have stalked away except that he grasped her wrist, and that brought her to her senses. Perhaps it was his intention after all to make her an object of scandal, but she would not play into his hands.

She looked at him and smiled. The music struck up and she placed her hand upon his shoulder.

He took her right hand in his left and placed his other at her waist, looking at her as if she were an unexploded bomb. They began to dance.

Perhaps it was the glittering room and the fine company, but the waltz had never been like this before. It had been danced in Lincolnshire—greatly daring—at informal hops and the occasional assembly, but Amy had always preferred the country dances. They were more fun.

Now, spinning in Harry's Crisp's arms, surrendering to his direction, trusting to his skill, she felt the magic touch her and knew why so many were still scandalized by it. Such rapturous feelings must be wrong.

She was irresistibly carried back to their short time of harmony—shared laughter, kindness, a kiss—but when she looked up at him, he was a stranger.

She wished the mask would fall and reveal the man she had spent that afternoon with, he in shirtsleeves, she in a blanket. Though there could be no future for them, could they not be friends? Reviewing their path to this bitter point, she had to admit that a great deal of it had been her fault. Her feelings had frightened her, and she had lost control and struck out to drive him away.

She made a decision and forced out the words. "I'm sorry."

"For what?" he asked coolly, not even looking at her. "You dance as beautifully as anyone would expect."

"For being intolerably rude," she persisted. "If that is how you see it."

He glanced down and raised a brow. "Is not that how you see it?"

Amy kept a hold on her temper. "Perhaps. But chiefly, I was being honest," she said.

"So was I."

"When?" she asked, confused.

"When I called you a bitch." He smiled and executed a particularly dizzy turn.

Amy gasped and tried to pull out of his arms, but he was too strong for her. "Going to hit me again?" he asked through a tight smile. "Not here, you're not."

"I wouldn't put myself to the trouble," snapped Amy, giving up the struggle and refusing to look at him. "Your manners are beyond correction."

"Was that what you were trying to do? You might try to teach by example the next time."

"There will be no next time."

"Ah, no," he said. "Both Forbes and Rowanford have excellent manners, I'm sure. I think I'll set up a book on which one you'll pick. Are you willing to give up a few hundred thousand in ready cash for a coronet, or is it really just the money that counts?"

Amy refused to speak to him, though she remembered to keep a small, tight smile on her face.

"Of course Rowanford also has the advantage of being childless," he carried on. "Sir Cedric's hopeful offspring will doubtless cut up rough at seeing the family fortune trickling through your fingers. Have you got into it already? Such fine feathers, and a very pretty necklace."

The music ended, thank God. Amy would have walked away, but he took a grip on her arm, which she couldn't break, and said, "I will, of course, escort you to your aunt."

As they approached Aunt Lizzie, Amy said, "You understand, of course, that I will never agree to dance with you again, Mr. Crisp."

His smile was chilly as he bowed. "My dear Amethyst, you will never be asked."

With willpower she had never before been aware of, Amy smiled as he walked away, and as she took a seat by her aunt.

"I was never so surprised!" declared Lizzie. "Fancy you standing up with him and acting as if you were nothing but casual acquaintances."

"That is all we are," said Amy, her jaw aching with the smile.

"With a proposal and a red face between you," said Lizzie skeptically. "Oh well, I never did think to understand you, Amethyst. Even in the cradle you were contrary. Now, what about that duke?"

"What about Sir Cedric?" countered Amy, looking around. She was in an excellent mood to bring the man to the point.

"He was dancing with Nell. Really, Amethyst. You *can't* turn your nose up at a duke. He's warm enough—I've made inquiries. Think what it would be for your sisters and Jasper to be related to a duke."

Oh heavens, thought Amy. She'd never thought of the power of connections. Was it her duty to weigh title against cash just as Harry Crisp had implied? She had no time to consider it, for her next partner came to claim her, and after that was the supper dance.

She knew the fact that the duke was standing up with her for the second time was being noticed. She supposed he was the catch of the Season and she really should make some effort to reel him in. She even liked him, for he seemed thoroughly pleasant for such an exalted personage.

She spent most of the dance pondering her reluctance

to try to snare Rowanford. She decided it was that it wouldn't be fair to cheat such a man out of the warmth he deserved, and she felt no particular warmth for him. Sir Cedric was a simpler case and would be content with what she had to offer.

Having made up her mind, Amy was anxious to be back in her prospective husband's company.

When she and Rowanford entered the supper room, however, Clyta noisily summoned them over to her table, and Amy felt obliged to go. This was, after all, why she was here. She spotted Sir Cedric at another table with Clyta's parents, Nell, Lizzie, and another gentleman. She gave a little wave and told herself she wished she were at that table. Honesty compelled her to admit, however, that such a middle-aged group looked extremely dull. It was a little daunting to think that such groupings would be her natural setting as Lady Forbes.

Clyta's supper partner was Harry, and he was sitting at the head of the small oval table. Chart Ashby was there with a dark-haired beauty who was introduced as Lucy Frogmorton. Amy and Rowanford took the two vacant seats, and Amy found herself between the duke and Chart but directly opposite Harry.

She immediately turned her attention away to her right side. "Do you come to London every year, Mr. Ashby?" she asked as she forked a morsel of tender poached salmon.

"A week or two, perhaps, Miss de Lacy," he said with bland courtesy. "This year I'm fixed here for the Season, helping Harry to choose a wife."

Amy found the salmon stuck in her throat so that she feared she would choke. She managed to get it down and took a quick drink of wine to help it. "Er . . . that should not be difficult," she said, hoping she sounded blasé.

"No," he said with a slanting look at her. "What woman would refuse him?"

Amy swallowed against a dry throat. This man disliked her for what she had done to his friend.

After a moment anger came to her rescue. What had she done, after all? On only a few hours' acquaintance, the man had had the effrontery to propose marriage and then not take no for an answer. He had been abominably rude and she had reacted to that.

"Tastes vary, Mr. Ashby," she said coolly, "otherwise all this strutting and preening would not be necessary. We could all just draw lots."

"And are you strutting or preening, Miss de Lacy?" he asked, but she thought she saw a glint of reluctant admiration in his eyes.

"Oh, both. And you?"

"I'm not on the lookout for a wife, so I don't have to bother. I'm merely protecting my friend from scheming harpies. May I help you to some sauce, Miss de Lacy?"

Amy prayed she wasn't blushing, but feared she was. She refused the sauce, then asked sweetly, "Does he need protection? I would have thought Mr. Crisp able to stand up for himself."

"No man is impervious to all attacks, I fear."

"Of what do you speak, Ashby?" asked the duke, turning away from Clyta. "It almost sounds like war. Not a subject for supper."

Amy turned gladly to her left, relieved to have the confrontation ended. She wondered briefly whether the conversation could be overheard from the other end of the table and what Harry Crisp was making of it. "Love and war are closely related, your grace," she said.

"So you were speaking of love," said the duke, and Amy was startled. *Had* she been speaking of love? "I hope you're wrong," he continued. "I hope to marry for love but fancy a peaceful life."

"Then don't marry Amy," said Clyta loudly. "She's always planning something or other."

Amy stared at her friend, hurt, but then realized the words had been innocent. It was true that at school she'd thought up some interesting pranks and adventures. A quick glance around the table showed her that Chart and Harry had taken it wrongly. "What are you suggesting, Clyta?" she asked lightly.

"Well I swear," said Clyta, unaware of undercurrents,

"we would all have been perfectly content with a simple picnic at Lord Forster's if you hadn't conceived the notion to invade his orchard and have an apple fight."

Amy couldn't help but grin at the memory. "They were only windfalls."

"But Miss Lindsay had the vapors and Miss Mallory was not amused. And," went on Clyta, "what about the night you climbed out of your room down a rope of sheets, for a dare?"

"I wanted to see if it could be done," said Amy, lost in memory.

"Planning an elopement, perhaps?" asked Harry dryly.

Amy came back to reality with a bump.

"Oh no," said Clyta. "That was Chloe." She was referring to her older sister.

"Chloe eloped from home, not school," said Chart pointedly, "and there was no need of ropes. Stop waving our dirty linen in public, Clyta."

She looked abashed but said, "I don't consider Chloe dirty linen, Chart. And it all worked out in the end. Oh!"

It was clear to Amy at least that Chart had just kicked his sister under the table. It seemed a bit nonsensical. The whole world knew Chloe Ashby had eloped at seventeen with a scoundrel who broke his neck in a driving accident. She had since made a wiser, better marriage.

The duke said to Amy, "So you are a prankster, Miss de Lacy."

"I have outgrown such foolishness, your grace."

He smiled. "What a shame."

"Oh, don't worry, Rowanford," said Harry smiling coolly at Amy. "Pranksters probably grow up to be full-fledged adventurers. Or, I suppose, adventuresses."

"Oh no," said Miss Frogmorton blandly. "You cannot mean that, Mr. Crisp. An adventuress is not a proper thing to call a lady."

"Of course, Miss Frogmorton," said Harry. "You are quite correct." His eyes clashed with Amy's for a moment before he turned to address some remark to Miss Frogmorton.

Amy saw how very warmly the young woman smiled

at him, how she lowered her lashes and peeped up at him, and how he laid a hand over hers for a moment, summoning a convenient and very becoming blush. Amy's hand hurt, and she realized her grip was bruisingly tight on her fork. She relaxed it and wrenched her attention away.

Clyta was talking with great animation to the duke. Amy was not sure this boded well—heaven knows what she was saying—but it forced her to turn warily back to Chart Ashby.

"This is a lovely house," she said. "Does the duke entertain here often?"

"Very rarely," he said. "My uncle is in frail health and my cousin, the Marquess of Chelmly, has little taste for London. He stays here when he comes to town on business but doesn't entertain."

"It seems a shame," said Amy, meaning that the mansion was so rarely used.

"That he doesn't like London?" queried Chart. "I suppose it does disappoint you that he is not accessible. But you have to admit, being prime quarry in this jungle is enough to put anyone off. Rowanford," he said across the table, "do you ever feel like donning armor before venturing to a Society function? Some of these young ladies would stop at nothing to squeeze an offer of marriage out of you."

The conversation swirled off into some of the more outlandish tricks attempted by desperate young ladies. When Rowanford described one hopeful's maneuver of having her coach break down at his gates, Amy could feel her face heat. She looked up and her eyes were trapped by Harry Crisp's; she seemed to be unable to do anything about it. He looked puzzled rather than angry.

Amy forced herself to look away, and she saw that Clyta looked close to tears.

Why? Surely Clyta couldn't realize how uncomfortable this topic made Amy. Though Amy was very fond of her friend, she did not think Clyta particularly perceptive.

Then Amy saw the way Clyta was looking at Rowanford and had a flash of inspiration. Clyta loved him. Doubtless she was hunting him in her own fashion and would assume all this laughter was addressed at her, even though she would never think of using these conniving tricks.

No wonder Clyta had reacted so stridently to the idea that Amy might be a contender for the duke's hand. She was doubtless wishing she'd never invited Amy to the ball.

Amy felt the familiar sickness creep over her, the disgust at her own looks and the effect they could have on both women and men. Unlike some of the other girls at school, Clyta had never minded being with Amy, for she was good-looking herself, of unassailably high rank, and had never been given to envy. Now it was different. Now there was something Clyta wanted, and Amy might be the enemy.

As soon as she saw the opportunity, Amy deflected the conversation into less painful paths. She saw Harry Crisp note her maneuver but shrugged it off. To Hades with him, she thought impatiently. It was Clyta's feelings that were important.

After the meal, she went with Clyta to the ladies' withdrawing room, wondering how to set her friend's mind at rest without revealing that she knew her secret.

Clyta's hair was losing some of the blue ribbons wound in it, and a maid set about repairs.

"You're a great success, Clyta," Amy said. "That gown is very becoming."

"Mama has excellent taste," said Clyta flatly.

"You will soon have a procession of suitors and be prostrated by the effort of choosing between them."

The joking tone got through to Clyta and she smiled a little. "More likely you, I would think, Amy."

"Me?" said Amy, pleased to have worked an opening. "Oh, I doubt it. After all, I haven't a penny to my name, and I don't intend to be coming to more of these events. Besides," she said, leaning close and lowering her voice, "I have great hopes of an offer from Sir Cedric."

Clyta stared. "But he's old enough to be your father!"

Amy tried to look enchanted with her fate. "I like a mature man."

The maid finished and they left the room to return to the ballroom. In the corridor, Clyta stopped and hesitantly asked, "Do you mean that if someone younger were to offer for you—someone like Rowanford, for example—you would turn him down?"

Heavens, thought Amy, Clyta was guileless as a baby. Amy feared for her in this silken jungle. Unfortunately she couldn't imagine her winning her heart's desire, even without competition, but all she could do was make sure that competition was not herself. "The duke wouldn't offer for a penniless creature such as I," she said briskly, "and he would probably look for higher birth, too. It seems to me that dukes tend to marry into other ducal families."

"Do you think so?" asked Clyta, brightening. "But if he did offer?" she persisted. "After all, there were the Gunning sisters."

"If Rowanford were to offer," said Amy firmly, "I would not accept." They entered the ballroom, where selections from *Così fan tutte* were being sung by part of the company from the Royal Opera. Amy leaned close to Clyta's ear. "If you don't mind, Clyta, I would like to join Sir Cedric over there."

Clyta turned a brilliant smile on her. "Of course not, dearest." She even squeezed her hand. "Good luck."

As Amy wove her way across the room, she tried to think of ways to help Clyta snare the Duke of Rowanford, and failed. Clyta had her fair share of the family's handsome looks, and when at ease and natural she was possessed of an innocent charm, but she was not showing at all well in Society. Even if the duke were looking for a bride—and he was on the young side, being surely of an age with Chart Ashby and Harry Crisp—there was little reason for his choice to fall on Clyta.

And yet Chart Ashby had said that Harry Crisp was looking for a bride. Amy stopped dead.

He'd produced that abrupt offer after the slightest of

acquaintance. Had he just been trying to get a bride with as little trouble as possible? And for that he'd put her through this torture of self-recrimination and exposed her to the taunting of his friends?

She wished she had the rejecting of him to do all over again!

She saw Nell, Lizzie, and Sir Cedric and eased in next to them. Sir Cedric's welcoming smile did seem very warm and admiring. Amy smiled back as brilliantly as she knew how. *Ask me, Sir Cedric. Ask me now. Then I can go home and never see Harry Crisp again, at least not until I'm safely married.*

Sir Cedric was kind and attentive for the remainder of the ball, but he said nothing particular. Amy pinned her hopes on tomorrow's visit to his home.

# =11=

Sɪʀ Cᴇᴅʀɪᴄ's ʜᴏᴜsᴇ was very fine. It was new, with snowy white stucco, large, gleaming windows, and a fine garden. He invited his guests to stroll with him down the length of the garden to the orchard, but only Amy accepted. Lizzie and Nell preferred to rest on chairs on the lawn close to the house.

As Amy and Sir Cedric passed a yew hedge so they were out of sight of her chaperons, her heart began to beat faster. Was this the moment?

"How lovely this is," she said.

"I do not keep up a country property, Miss de Lacy, having little time for it, and so I like to have the country here in London."

"One could almost think oneself in the country, Sir Cedric." Amy felt she was gushing but the comment was true. The large garden, with flowers, fruit trees, and vegetables was surrounded by a high wall, which cut out the bustle of the city. The place seemed extraordinarily full of bees and butterflies, as if they recognized the haven it represented.

"I think you miss the country, my dear."

"Yes," said Amy, only then realizing that this wasn't the right answer for someone who had just admitted that he rarely went there. She went on quickly, "But that is largely because I have always lived in the country."

"So you are enjoying London?"

"Oh yes. There are so many new things to see and do."

"And when you have done them all?" he asked.

Amy felt rather as if she were being interrogated, but she smiled at him. "Was it not Dr. Johnson who said, 'When a man is tired of London, he is tired of life?' I assure you I am not tired of life yet, Sir Cedric."

He laughed, "I should hope not, young lady. You have your life spread before you like a magic carpet. You are made for balls and other festivities. You should enjoy them to the full while you are here."

That "while you are here" sounded ominous. "But I expect to be here for a long time," she said firmly.

He made no response, but changed direction so they were returning to the house. Amy felt desperate. This was surely the point at which a true fortune hunter would act to save the day. She reviewed the stories told the night before but couldn't bring herself to use any of the techniques described. She didn't believe she could swoon into his arms, and she would die rather than rip her clothing and cry rape.

She made one try. "You must be lonely living in this big house all by yourself, Sir Cedric."

"But I don't," he responded. "My oldest son and his family live here with me. It will, after all, be his one day. I hope . . . ah, yes." They passed back through the yew hedge, and Amy saw that her chaperons had been joined by a family.

A severe-looking man in the knee breeches commonly worn for business sat by a quiet, pleasant-looking woman who was clearly expecting another child. A toddler and a boy of about five played nearby under the eye of a nursemaid.

Amy was introduced to Edwin Forbes and his wife Susan. Mrs. Forbes seemed pleasant enough, but her husband was chilly. It might just be his nature, for he had a cool demeanor, but Amy suspected he disliked his father's association with her, and with reason.

Amy looked guiltily at the two charming children and felt as if she were planning to steal the bread from their mouths. It did no good to remind herself that Sir Cedric was reputed to be enormously rich; anything she gained for her family would be taken from his.

But she must. She had no choice. She could not go home empty handed.

She thought briefly of the Duke of Rowanford. He was wealthy enough and free of entanglements. But even if he could be brought to the point, he wanted to marry for love. Nor could she contemplate stealing Clyta's beloved, even if she could find no way to help her friend to gain him. Better he marry another entirely.

Amy tried to be gay and charming as the tea progressed, but the effort exhausted her and she subsided into silence, giving thanks for Nell Claybury who filled the gap with effortlessly pleasant chatter.

As she parted from Sir Cedric at the coach, Amy looked anxiously for some indication of his feeling. His smile was very kind, and he squeezed her hand slightly before releasing it. She forced herself to relax. Just because she felt this pressing urgency was no reason for him to feel it. Indeed, he would doubtless believe it was too soon to be speaking. He had only known her for a fortnight and not everyone, she thought waspishly, was as crass as Harry Crisp.

"Sir Cedric is such a charming man, isn't he?" said Nell as they headed back to Chelsea. "His wife was a lovely woman, so warm and generous."

"How long ago did she die?" Amy asked.

Nell wrinkled her brow in thought. "It must be a few years. Before my Bertie, of that I'm sure. It was a long illness, I'm afraid. It must have been very difficult for them all. It is time he married again." She looked at Amy thoughtfully.

On their return to New Street, Amy found a letter from Beryl and a note from Clyta.

Beryl wrote:

*Dearest Amy,*
    *We are so pleased to hear of your adventures, and*

you mustn't feel guilty for enjoying yourself. I am sure we will all have our turn at dissipation once you are married. Nor must you be in a hurry about such an important decision. You must be sure to choose the man who will truly make you happy.

Heavens. Beryl seemed to think they were lining up at the door.

We are all well and, yes, we are remembering to water the vegetables and I have sown another crop of peas and beans. I laugh to think of you at a grand ball worrying about whether we have earthed up the potatoes. I am sure your conversation is extraordinary, but will doubtless charm an agriculturally minded gentleman!

Mr. Staverley invited us over again to consider his plans for the acolyte's cell, for we are convinced that is what it is. He has ordered a great many books on the subject and is in daily expectation of a visit from Sir Arnold Foulks-Hamilton, the antiquarian, who will surely be able to give a definitive assessment. I fear poor Mr. Staverley will be upset if the building does not prove to be monastic, but I am convinced it must be.

He was most disappointed that you were away. I took Jassy for convention's sake but it did not serve, for she was bored and restless, so I think I will go alone next time. Do you think that too bold? I told him a little of your triumphs and I am sure it piqued his interest. So if your London beaux are not to your liking perhaps you should give Mr. Staverley another chance. I am convinced he is shy. Though he does not advertise the fact I believe he was born a tradesman's son and has made himself. I think the better of him for it.

The only problem I have to relate is that the pig seems very out of sorts whenever either I or Jassy feed him. (It does not surprise me that he misses you as *much as we all do.) He eventually settles to his feed but there is a great deal of squealing at first, as if he is in pain. Do you have any advice?*

*Wave at the tsar for us, dearest.*

*Your loving sister, Beryl.*

Amy chuckled, rather misty eyed. She'd go odds they wouldn't earth up the potatoes high enough, especially if Beryl had her head in a book on medieval architecture. She feared Mr. Staverley was taking advantage of Beryl's generous nature but it was providing diversion, which was something.

As for poor Augustus . . .

Amy sat at the writing desk and gave a cheerful account of her activities, especially Clyta's ball, for Beryl would like that. She made no mention of Harry Crisp, and only passing reference to Sir Cedric. She wanted Beryl to be prepared for the news when it came, but did not want to raise her hopes too high in case nothing came of it.

She paused and worried the end of the quill with her teeth. It *must*. It *must*.

She briskly dipped the pen in the well. "As for Augustus," she wrote, "I fear he may have a delicate digestion. I find a whole apple or carrot with his food seems to stimulate his system. Failing that, a large hunk of stale bread or even cake if available. This may seem indulgent, but I fear it is necessary if he is to fatten up adequately for . . ." Amy had to brace herself to write the words, ". . . slaughtering day."

A tear rolled down her cheek. She only just whipped the paper away before it fell. More splashed to the desk, one after the other. She gulped and swallowed them, then wiped at her eyes. She *couldn't* be weeping over a pig!

But she wasn't. She was weeping over herself, for her own slaughtering day approached.

She forced herself to contemplate roast pork, plump sausages, crunchy-crust pie. That, however, reminded her of the Melton pie she had shared in the kitchen of Coppice Farm, with Harry Crisp sitting across from her, smiling, and confessing that he wasn't truly mad about hunting.

He had talked to her easily and honestly. She had never really been honest with him, except when she had told him she would marry for money. This was tragic, when he was the one person with whom she might be able to share her thoughts.

Oh, damnation! Amy blew her nose, sealed the letter, and picked up Clyta's, praying it was a cheerful message.

*Dear Amy,*

*We are planning a jaunt to Lord Templemore's estate, Maiden Hall. (I overheard my mother comment that a less appropriate name for his residence was hard to imagine. My father was unwise enough to say that he didn't doubt any number of maidens had passed through the door. You can imagine the fireworks! I was very nearly forbidden to go, but Chart and Randal both weighed in to assure Mama he is a reformed man now that he is married. I am a little disappointed. Gossip has always painted a very intriguing picture and I saw him at Randal's wedding. Quel beau! I could imagine his fatal attraction.)*

*We very much want you to join us. Rowanford says he is going to call and ask you, and will provide a mount. Please say yes, otherwise I'm not sure he will join the party.*

*I know I gave myself away last night, dear friend. I fear I am no hand at dissembling. I doubt I have a chance to attach his interest, but I must make a push. I fear he is too used to regarding me as an awkward younger sister, just like all Chart's friends.*

*I do show well on a horse, though.*

*In case you have not brought a habit to Town, I have had Melrose take up the hem on my spare one and sent it over, along with a spare pair of boots. We always were of a size, except for a couple of inches of height.*

*Please, please, please agree, Amy.*
*Your dearest friend,*
*Clyta.*

Amy sighed.

"Bad news, dear?" asked Nell Claybury as she entered. Amy feared her tears had left a mark.

"Not really," she said with a smile. "It is just Clyta Ashby asking me to join a riding party. Or at least, forewarning me that Rowanford is going to invite me."

Nell looked unconvinced that this was the whole story but said, "That is wonderful, Amy. Just what you need."

"I told you I have no wish to move in high circles," Amy said. "And I may have other invitations."

"If you mean Sir Cedric," said Nell, causing Amy to blush, "did you not hear him say that he will be out of Town for a few days?"

That must have been while she was daydreaming. Amy felt a mixture of frustration and relief at the news.

"So there is no reason," Nell continued, "for you not to enjoy yourself. What harm can it do if you spend a pleasant afternoon with your friends?"

None at all, thought Amy, except that she feared Harry Crisp would be one of the group.

But she wanted to go. It was over two years since she had ridden a decent horse. Why the devil should she let Harry Crisp keep her from such a treat? He could stay home if the situation bothered him.

"Lord save us!" declared Nell, startling Amy out of her thoughts. "Do you mean the Duke of Rowanford is going to come *here?*"

"I think so," said Amy. To her amazement, sensible Nell Claybury was transformed before her eyes into a bundle of anticipation and nerves, dashing around to make sure every corner of the house was perfect, and lamenting the fact that she did not keep a butler who would be knowledgeable about wines.

In the end she sent the footman to her friend, Jerome Irons, the wine merchant, begging him to send over a selection of fine wines suitable for immediate drinking. Within half an hour four clerks arrived bearing the bottles with great care, so as to avoid disturbing them, and left them along with careful instructions for their correct handling.

"Bertie always looked after the wines," said Nell nervously. "I have no palate at all—the cheapest wine tastes as good as the most expensive, so I don't bother myself over much. Am I acting the fool?" she asked ruefully.

Amy smiled. "Not at all. A duke is a duke, after all. I just hope you don't mind him coming here. I'm causing you a great deal of bother."

"Not a bit of it," said Nell. "I was bored to death before you came. I'm having a wonderful time."

And indeed, thought Amy, that was surely the truth. Nell was looking brighter and younger day by day. Amy told her so, adding, "I expect we will have your suitors beating down the door as well as mine." She was amused when Nell blushed, and wondered just who the promising gentleman might be.

Francis, the footman, looked puffed up with pride when he ushered the duke into Nell's drawing room, and the maid who helped bring in the tea tray appeared ready to drop it with nerves. Aunt Lizzie had the complacent look of one who says to herself, "I told you so."

Rowanford must be aware of the effect he was having—Amy wondered if he found it tiresome to be set apart so young merely by a title—but he put on no airs and graces. He soon had Nell at her ease. He was a thoroughly pleasant man.

Again the thought came to Amy that she could surely induce the appropriate degree of warmth for him in her heart if she tried, and she certainly wasn't above the idea that marrying the duke would be a glorious triumph. But then she remembered Clyta. It wouldn't do. And the simple fact was that it might be possible to make oneself fall in love, but only when the heart was free.

Amy was having to accept that her heart was not free.

Rowanford turned to her and delivered the expected invitation. Amy hesitated. Her acceptance might encourage him, and she knew she was going to be thrown together with Harry. Perhaps it might be wiser to say no.

On the other hand, she wanted to go, and perhaps she could find a way to promote Clyta's cause. Sir Cedric would be out of town, so she needn't feel guilty.

The old saying came to mind—While the cat's away, the mice will play. That wasn't the right sort of thing to think at all.

Then she recalled Nell saying, "So there is no reason for you not to enjoy yourself," as if she did not expect Amy to have true pleasure with Sir Cedric. Amy looked at Nell with dismay. That was nonsense, surely.

"Amy, dear," said Nell. "Are you all right?"

Amy collected her wits. "I'm sorry." She turned to Rowanford. "That is very kind of you, your grace. If you can provide the mount, I will be delighted to join the party. But please make the horse a gentle one. I am somewhat out of practice."

His smile was exceedingly warm. "Don't worry, Miss de Lacy. I will take the greatest care of you."

As he left, Amy realized he had taken her confusion as being the result of her feelings at receiving such a flattering invitation. He might be a thoroughly pleasant man, but he was a duke. He had apparently inherited during his school days, so it was not surprising that he have a high opinion of his own importance.

She feared she had paved the way for yet further complications in her life.

Two days later, Amy waited the arrival of the party, dressed in Clyta's rich red habit, and tremulous with the hope that Harry Crisp would be present.

It was stupid, it was wrong, but she was rapidly losing control of her feelings. She was glad Sir Cedric was away, as if she had been let out of prison. She wanted to see Harry and be with him as happily and warmly as they had been in the farm kitchen.

She knew that was impossible, but she would see him. At least she would see him.

It was Rowanford who came to the door, and who tossed Amy into the saddle of the rather solid gray he had brought for her. She gave a general, cheery greeting, her eyes passing over Harry without pause, but catching an impression she held in her heart. She hadn't clearly noted who else was present.

As they set out, she was aware of him riding behind, but as her feelings steadied, she took in the party. Harry was behind, she knew, riding with that dark-haired girl from Clyta's ball—Lucy Frogmorton.

He was going to marry her. It must be so if he was singling her out in such a fashion. She shouldn't begrudge him his happiness, but she did.

Ahead in the lead were Lord Randal and his wife, behind them Chart and Clyta. Clyta waved back cheerfully.

Amy remembered her purpose. "Clyta and I were great friends at school," she said to the duke. "She has a wonderfully warm heart."

"Yes," he said carelessly. "A pretty good sort. Doesn't make a fuss over things."

"And very pretty," Amy continued. "I'm sure she'll make an excellent match." Was she laying it on a bit thick? It was clear, however, that she would need a bludgeon to make an impression upon his mind.

"Clyta?" he said, looking at the subject of the conversation. "She's got a fine seat. All the Ashbys are bruising riders. How do you find your mount, Miss de Lacy?"

Amy found it a slug. It was clear Rowanford had taken her caution too seriously. This horse would be ideal for a nonequestrian grandmother. "I feel very safe," she said.

"Excellent. I shall take good care of you, Miss de Lacy. Have no fear."

Amy sighed and wished there was a convenient piece

of furniture to heft to prove she was not as fragile as she appeared.

It was not too bad as long as they were on the city streets, but they were soon in countryside and the pace began to quicken. Amy's mount quickened, but not nearly as much as the others. This was made worse by the duke saying that they must hold back for Miss de Lacy's sake, as if she were scared to canter.

In the end, as when she had returned home from the Coneybears, the rest of the party took side trips while she ambled along, trying to pretend she was content. Even Rowanford abandoned her at times, though someone always kept her company.

She suddenly found Lord Randal by her side. "Is this pace really the best you can do?"

There was something in his eyes that brought out an honest answer. "It is the best this horse can do. But don't say anything. The duke will be hurt."

He grinned. "I am an authority on dukes. A duke's self-esteem can only be dented by a grenade." He put two fingers in his mouth like a barrow-boy and whistled. His wife waved and rode back.

"You," he said as soon as she arrived, "are in need of a rest."

"Hardly," she replied.

He ignored this. "Miss de Lacy has kindly agreed to let you borrow this placid, gentle beast for a while. I'm sure you are grateful."

"Oh no," Amy protested, but was overridden.

"How kind," said Sophie. "I'm sure I am in need of a rest. Married life," she said faintly, with a sliding look at her husband, "is *so* exhausting."

He was fighting laughter as he dismounted and assisted them in the exchange, adjusting the stirrup leathers. By this time the rest of the party had gathered.

"Is something the matter?" Rowanford asked.

"Sophie needs a rest," said Randal, causing looks of astonishment from all except the duke, "and Miss de Lacy has agreed it would do her good to be a bit more venturesome. Perhaps you could stay with Sophie for a little while, Rowanford, while I see how Miss de Lacy does."

He gave the duke no chance to object but led the way into a piece of light woodland. Amy happily followed. Lady Randal's black thoroughbred was a marvelous piece of horseflesh. They were soon traveling the wide bridle paths at a canter.

He grinned at her. "All right?"

"Of course! I only meant I was a little out of practice, not that I was unable to ride entirely."

There was a log lying across the path ahead. "Game?" he asked.

Amy nodded and they both sailed over it. She laughed.

He slowed his mount down. "We mustn't tire them. There's a way to go. If we head this way it should bring us back to the road." As the pace steadied he said, "You ride well."

Amy looked at him. "I was raised in the Shires, Lord Randal."

He laughed. "I suppose you were. And the Belvoir used to meet at Stonycourt, didn't it? I remember attending there."

Amy nodded. "In better days."

They rode on, hooves muffled by the soft leaf mold, seeming alone among the trees in heavy green leaf.

Suddenly he spoke. "There are more important things in life than money, you know."

Amy was shocked by the attack. "There speaks someone who has never been without."

"True," he acknowledged. "But my comment is still valid. No one can survive without food and shelter, but I would give up almost everything for Sophie."

Amy knew what he was saying, and it was unfair, but she couldn't say so. "We are all different, I suppose, my lord."

They had come to the road, and the party was some way behind.

"I wonder," he said, then called to the others.

# ═12═

THEY SPEEDED UP and soon the party was all together again. Amy insisted on changing horses and soon found herself partnered with the duke.

"I am sorry the horse is too slow for you," he said stiffly.

Amy was about to be conciliatory when she realized that she might serve Clyta's case better if she could keep his feathers ruffled. "It is a little placid, your grace," she said. "I was raised in hunting country and am used to spirited mounts."

He turned distinctly cool. "Perhaps Templemore will be able to offer you an exchange for the return." At the earliest opportunity he jumped his gray into a nearby meadow for a gallop. Randal and Sophie were already gone. Chart and Miss Frogmorton were ahead. When Clyta and Harry moved to follow the duke, Amy saw her chance and called out, "Mr. Crisp!"

He turned, startled, then waved Clyta on and came back.

Clyta flashed Amy a grateful smile and set off after the duke. Amy had acted on impulse, but now she was faced with the problem of what to say to her rejected suitor.

"Yes, Miss de Lacy," he said warily as his horse came alongside hers.

Amy badly wanted him to smile at her. "I wish we could put an end to the ill feelings between us, sir."

He raised his brows. "Ill feelings?" he queried. "I would say we disliked one another intensely."

Amy swallowed and stared between her horse's ears. "I don't dislike you."

When she risked a look at him, he seemed sober. "Don't you? You're very tolerant of insults then."

"You insulted me and I hit you. That should wipe the slate clean."

He appeared skeptical. "What's the matter? Are all your other suitors failing you, Miss de Lacy? You have just mishandled Rowanford, but don't despair. You can doubtless get him back with a smile or two."

"I don't want Rowanford," said Amy sharply, "and if you were to ask me again to marry you I would again say no. I do have thoughts other than marital!" She moderated her tone. "I just wish we could be more at ease."

"Why?"

Amy looked away. It was an excellent question. "I don't know."

They rode for a while in silence, then he said, "So it's to be the banker. You surprise me. Rowanford's nearly as rich, and there is no comparison in other respects."

"Sir Cedric is an estimable man."

"Yes," he said dryly. "He'd make you an excellent father."

Amy looked at him. "It is not unusual for there to be a disparity of ages in marriage."

"But not desirable. It will be a foolish match. He's not an old man in need of an heir, and I doubt he wants a new young family to add to his grown one. What have you in common? Ah, I forgot," he said with what could almost be a touch of humor, "you share an interest in steam engines."

Amy's lips twitched in response. "I'm afraid not." He *was* teasing her. Her heart swelled in response, and she only wanted to keep him here beside her in harmony. "Do you think there is anything in it?"

"Steam?" he said. "Assuredly. Steam pumps have been in use in mining for decades, and now steam carriages on rails haul coal at a number of mines. Steam boats are widely used in the Americas, and there is one on the

Clyde, I believe. You must know this, however," he said with a distinctly humorous glance at her. "You were at Mr. Boyd's lecture."

Amy bit her lip. "I was present, yes. I did think," she added hurriedly, "that the powerful effect of steam was clearly demonstrated. I wondered if it could be put to domestic use."

"Cleaning, washing, and such like?" he asked, intrigued. "I suppose a steam mechanism could move a scrubbing brush backward and forward, or agitate washing. But steam engines are too large."

"Could they not be made smaller?"

"It should be looked into. It is a dangerous notion," he pointed out with a smile. "If machines do the cleaning, the servants will be idle, and you know what the devil does with idle hands."

Amy shared his amusement, but then had a disquieting thought. Their harmony felt as fragile as a cobweb, and she hated to break it with one of her gloomy, sensible predictions but she could not help it. "More dangerous than that," she said. "Would it not be like the new agricultural machines, and the power looms, which are throwing people out of work? If machines take over all the household work, what would the servants do? The poverty would be terrible."

He was not disgusted but nodded thoughtfully. "Good point. Perhaps we'd better not share our inspiration with the world, then. Poverty creates all kinds of havoc."

Amy felt the heat in her cheeks, but she did not look away. Did that refer to her and did he perhaps understand her predicament? "Poverty is terrible," she agreed. "It strips away dignity and leaves no time and energy for pleasure."

"Employment doesn't leave much time and energy for pleasure either," he pointed out. "Nor does it necessarily preclude poverty. Perhaps our machines would be useful after all if they made the servants' lives easier."

Amy was confused. Perhaps he hadn't been referring to her lack of money. Whatever his motives, she was entranced to find that he did not shy away from a serious topic, or appear shocked to find she had some thoughts of her own. "Some people expect their servants to work morn till night," she said. "If machines could do some of the work, they would simply hire fewer and expect more of the ones that remained."

"Is that what you would do?"

"No," said Amy with a sigh. "I would love to have the money to hire ample staff, and clothe and feed them well, and give them generous days off." She looked at him frankly. "A taste of menial labor would make us all better masters and mistresses."

He reached down to take her rein and stop her horse. "Miss de Lacy," he said somberly, "if you had accepted my offer you would have been mistress of a handsome estate, with yet greater to come in time. I would happily have provided ample funds for your generous rule. Did this not occur to you?"

"No," said Amy honestly, for such thoughts had not come into it that day. Had she thought at all?

"And now it has been pointed out?" he asked carefully.

Amy's heart constricted painfully. Was it all to do again? Nothing had really changed except now her fortune was within grasp, not hypothetical. "Now," she said woodenly, "I am going to marry Sir Cedric."

"My felicitations." He dropped her reins and set his horse in motion again.

Amy held her horse back and let him go. She felt sick. After all that had gone before he would have asked her again, given the smallest encouragement. His feelings perhaps ran as deep as hers and it could not be. Not when Sir Cedric and his millions were as good as hers.

But the thought that she was hurting Harry as much as she was hurting herself was close to unbearable. If there had been any sense to turning back and fleeing the rest of the day she would have done it, but Lord Randal was already riding back to see why she was just sitting there. She saw the others turn in some gates. At least they had arrived. She kicked her sluggard mount into a trot and followed.

Maiden Hall was an old house, a timbered Elizabethan sprawl in which few of the verticals or horizontals were straight. Riotously flowering borders surrounded it, backed by tall hollyhocks and delphiniums, and old-fashioned roses scrambled over the uneven surfaces on trellises.

The whole house seemed organic, growing out of the earth. It was beautiful and looked nothing like the home of a gazetted rake.

The rake himself lived up to Amy's expectations, however, when he came out to greet his guests. Tall, dark, handsome, and dressed with devastating informality in an open-necked shirt, sleeves rolled up to expose his arms like a laborer. No one could fail to be aware of a lithe body beneath the slight amount of clothing, and there was a wicked gleam in his eye even if he was supposed to have been tamed by matrimony.

Amy found it difficult to believe that the very ordinary woman by his side had achieved such a miracle. Lady Templemore was short and her gown was a simple green muslin. Her face was close to plain and her brown hair was gathered into a simple knot at the back.

But then she smiled at her guests and was beautiful. When she turned to her husband with a comment, she was dazzling, and the look in his eye showed he was tamed indeed, if devotion so heated could be called tame at all.

Amy looked over at Harry Crisp, who had dismounted to greet the Templemores. He would look at her like that, given the slightest encouragement. She'd seen the pale trace of it in his eyes that day in the kitchen, and the same, tightly controlled, just a little while ago. Perhaps he felt her eyes on his, for he turned, and after a hesitation came to assist her.

His eyes were shielded but could not hide his feelings. His hands burned at her waist as he lowered her. They lingered there far longer than necessary.

"I'm sorry," Amy said helplessly. "Oh dear. Why do I keep apologizing to you?"

He sighed with bleak humor. "Perhaps because you

are constantly at fault? I wonder what sins I committed in some previous existence to have encountered you, dear Amethyst."

She placed a hand on his arm. "Don't call me that, please."

He moved away, then held out his arm. "Come and be introduced to your hosts. You have something in common with Ver. He doesn't like his name either."

Amy was introduced to Lord and Lady Templemore, but when she made her curtsy and attempted to address them as such found Harry's words were true.

"If you wish to be invited here again,"the viscount said with a smile, "you will address me as Ver, and Emily as Emily. Outrageous, I know, but I have always been so and make it my practice to infect everyone I meet. So you won't feel uncomfortable, we will address you as Amy. Unless," he added with a distinctly wicked look, "you prefer Amethyst?"

Now, how did he even know her real name? Amy cast an alarmed look at Harry. Did the whole world know everything?

"You forget, Amy," said Verderan, offering an arm to lead her into the house, "Harry was staying at my hunting box when you had your contretemps with him."

Amy allowed herself to be led in, feeling as if she were being taken to court. Had she walked into a trap? It would not surprise her to find herself sat down and interrogated by all the friends of the man she was treating so cruelly.

Instead she was given into the hands of a maid, who showed her where she could take off her hat and refresh herself. The other women soon joined her.

Clyta took the opportunity to whisper, "Thank you. We rode together and he complimented my riding. I fear you offended Rowanford, though, by seeming dissatisfied with your mount."

"Indeed you did," said Miss Frogmorton snappily as she pushed at her perfect, glossy curls. Amy wondered if she was beginning to sense some threat to her pursuit of

Harry. "You would do better to learn a little decorum, Miss de Lacy, especially when having to admit to an address in *Chelsea*."

"I know all about decorum," said Amy coolly, "but I don't care a fig if I offend the duke."

Miss Frogmorton sneered. "Yes, my mother said you were on the catch for that rich old banker. Doubtless the best you can hope for from *Chelsea*. I think I begin to understand what Mr. Crisp meant about adventuresses."

She swept out before Clyta could get out a heated rebuttal. Amy merely stood tight lipped.

"Why that cat!" Clyta exploded.

"Not at all," said Amy. "It is perfectly true."

"No it isn't. You could have the duke if you made a push, and that's more than Lucy Frogmorton could."

Amy smiled and hugged her friend. "I always did love your loyalty, Clyta."

Sophie came in and ran a comb through auburn curls. "Miss Frogmorton looked as if she had just slain a dragon," she remarked.

"Just been rude you mean," said Clyta. "She was sneering at Amy just because she is living in Chelsea."

"It seemed a very pleasant part of Town," said Sophie lightly. "Perhaps Randal and I should move there and bring it into fashion." She assessed Amy. "It must be difficult being so uncomfortably beautiful." Without giving Amy a chance to comment, she linked arms with her. "Come along. Emily and I are completely secure in our husbands' affections and Clyta is your friend. The only envy you need fear here is from the green frog."

All three were giggling as they left the room.

After an ample luncheon, everyone walked out to explore the grounds of Maiden Hall. Amy found herself on the left arm of her host, with Sophie on his right. Emily balanced this by giving an arm each to Randal and Chart, while Clyta walked with Harry, and Lucy Frogmorton clung to the arm of the duke, looking extremely pleased with herself.

It was clear that Lucy had begun to aim higher than the future Lord Thoresby. Really, thought Amy, the girl was shameful. She cared nothing for feelings but was just out for the best catch she could land.

And how's that for a case of the pot calling the kettle black, Amy asked herself, but then reminded herself that she was seeking the greatest fortune for her family's sake, not her own.

"Despite what people think," said Verderan as they strolled between old yew hedges, "I did not name the place when I bought it. The name is ancient."

"But," asked Sophie naughtily, "didn't it add to the attractions just a little bit?"

"I still think Randal should beat you daily," he replied, with a look at Sophie which told Amy he was tamed in much the way a pet tiger is tamed—which is to say, not very much.

They had come to the end of the path and walked out into a meadow. Emily had brought some salt to feed the fallow deer which wandered beneath the nearby trees. She passed it out and the deer, for whom this was a familiar treat, pricked their way delicately to lip the food from their hands.

Amy offered some to a shy fawn and laughed with delight when it took it.

"And do you see just a piece of venison?"

Amy jerked round to face Harry. "Don't be horrible!"

"In what way is it different from the charming lamb?"

"Its mother is prettier."

He frowned slightly.

"Now what have I said?" Amy asked.

He grinned. "I've just remembered what Lucy Frogmorton's mother looks like."

Amy bit her lip and said, "Appearances are not everything, sir."

"True. But the woman also has a sheep's mind."

Amy gave him a reproving look. "Are you suggesting the deer are the epitome of intellectual wit? You are being deceived by appearances again."

He started as if suddenly brought back to himself. "So I am," he said and walked away.

Amy looked around and discovered Lord Randal had decided to emulate his friend and shed a great deal of clothing. As he was equally as handsome as Lord Templemore the effect was dramatic. Before her startled eyes Harry and Chart followed suit, shedding jackets and stocks and opening shirts to the breeze.

Neither had the lithe elegance of the older men but they were well built. Amy remembered thinking that she had never seen more of Harry's body than his face and hands, and she wished it had stayed that way.

The open shirt showed a glimpse of tawny curls on his chest, and there was a soft glint of them on his forearms. Amy discovered the desire to run her hand along those muscular arms was almost overpowering. She dragged her eyes away.

She stared over at Lord Templemore, who was laughing and looked a very Lucifer indeed. He had said, "I make it my practice to infect everyone I meet," and he'd been telling no less than the truth. A cricket ball had appeared from somewhere and he threw it hard and long to Chart, who caught it and threw it back. The man's body as he reached up to catch it was that of a thoroughbred, a hunting cat, sinuously graceful, dangerous.

He was not tamed at all. He was wicked, this place was wicked, and they were all being infected by it.

To prove Amy's point, Sophie shed the jacket of her habit, and pulled off her boots and stockings so she could join the game barefoot. Clyta giggled and followed suit.

"Oh dear," said Lucy Frogmorton looking aghast. "My mother . . ."

What they needed here, thought Amy, was a proper chaperone. Sophie, married lady though she was, was clearly no use. Lady Templemore was watching without a trace of unease. She came over to Amy and Lucy and said, "Don't you care to act like children? Very wise. Come and sit with me in the shade."

Amy trailed along but resentment grew in her. Where

was it written she could not join in this madness if she wanted to? A servant had brought cricket bats, and a game of sorts was taking place, though the rules were not ones that the Marylebone Cricket Club would recognize. Chart was currently chasing Lord Randal about with the ball.

The men's shirts were beginning to stick to their heated bodies. So were the lawn bodices of Sophie and Clyta's habits. Sophie had somehow pinned her skirt up so that it did not trail on the ground. A great deal of leg was exposed.

Lucy sat stiffly on a blanket in the shade of an oak and stared into the harmless distance. Lady Templemore was waiting for Amy.

"Why aren't you joining in?" Amy asked her.

"I'm increasing," Lady Templemore replied frankly. "I doubt one has to be as careful as they say, but Ver worries if I'm likely to fall or be hit." She gave a wistful sigh. "It's the very devil."

"Increasing?" asked Amy with a blush.

"Love," said the older woman. She looked shrewdly at Amy. "Why don't you join in? The sides are uneven."

Amy found she had her jacket, boots, and stockings off without conscious thought. She looked at her bare feet and remembered her time in Harry's kitchen. This was very, very dangerous, and if she had a particle of common sense she would dress again and watch the horizon with Lucy Frogmorton until sanity returned.

Common sense had deserted her.

"Here," said Lady Templemore and took a long pin from the etui which hung from her belt. "One learns to be prepared for anything," she commented. "It will be safer if your skirts don't trail." She went off to hitch up Clyta's skirts.

Amy did her best to pin up her skirts without revealing much leg. It proved impossible.

"This is terrible!" exclaimed Lucy, glaring at her. "My mother did question visiting such a place, but Mr. Crisp, and the duke . . ."

"Since you're here," said Amy, "don't you think you might as well join in? It can't do any harm."

Lucy stared at her. "It is as good as an orgy!"

Amy laughed as she went off to join in, but she thought Lucy made more sense than she knew. It wasn't an orgy and there was no chance that any true impropriety would take place, but it was wild and uncivilized. The laws of Society had been blown away as a brisk breeze dispels fog, and all sorts of outrageous things could happen.

There were no formal teams. Clyta and the duke were at bat and the rest were fielding. Lord Templemore placed Amy in right field a safe distance from the batters.

"I'm not afraid of a cricket ball, Lord Templemore," she said to him.

"Humor me," he replied. "Beauty such as yours should be preserved for a few years longer. And remember, it's Ver. You do want to be invited back, don't you?"

His shirt clung to him. His dark hair curled more madly than before and clung damply to his bare neck. Amy felt a dizziness that was nothing to do with him, except that he was bringing to life feelings she had thought not for her. "I don't know," she said, then added, "beauty is dangerous."

"You want to be invited back," he said firmly. "And beauty is a weapon. If you can't get rid of it, the least you can do is learn to use it appropriately."

Amy shivered as he walked away. She pushed her hands through her hair and felt that it, too, was damp. It doubtless had the same wildness as his. She looked down. Her bodice was already clinging to her breasts.

She looked toward Harry, who was stationed not far away. As if drawn he walked over to her.

"Do you know how to play?" he asked. His neck was so strong and brown and his chest was smoothly muscled.

"Yes," she said. "I'm quite good, actually, and I have a strong throwing arm."

He grinned, and his eyes were darker than usual. "I know that."

Amy felt herself heat up even more. "I am sorry for that."

"I'm not."

Amy thought it much wiser to turn her attention back to the game, though she was aware that he stayed by her instead of returning to his place. Sir Cedric, she reminded herself desperately. Sir Cedric and all the money they needed for Stonycourt, and horses, and luxuries, and dowries.

The ball came her way. She stopped it, but as she began to throw she realized her fashionable habit had sleeves too tight to allow a good throwing movement. With a muttered, "Drat," she tossed it to Harry and let him hurl it back to the bowler.

"I have a penknife in my pocket," he said. "I could cut your sleeves off. You have lovely arms, as I remember."

"I am lovely everywhere," she said tartly, using her beauty as a weapon, as Lord Templemore had suggested.

It did not drive Harry away. "I don't doubt it," he said. "I hope one day to have the evidence of my own eyes."

Amy stared at him. "You won't."

"Won't I?" he asked gently. "I wonder. I have decided to fight for you, Amethyst. You're everything I want in a wife—mind, body, and soul. And you're not indifferent. I knew it at Coppice Farm, and since then I've seen your eyes travel my body just as mine have traveled yours. You deserve better than an old man in your bed."

Amy turned away and closed her eyes. "Don't."

His voice could not be shut out. "I won't let you do this to yourself. I'm going to woo you, seduce you. If necessary, I'll abduct you."

Amy looked at him again. "You'd hang."

He smiled with hot, ravishing confidence. "Would you say you're sorry?"

The ball came their way again and he fielded it. Amy could no more have handled the ball than she could fly. "You're mad," she said dazedly. "I'm going to marry Sir Cedric."

"No you're not. You're going to marry someone you love. I hope that will be me."

Amy didn't know what to say in the face of such madness.

"If you're afraid of your family," he said gently, "I will protect you, Amy."

At last she found anger of sorts. "Of course I'm not afraid of my family. I love my family. Go away. How many times must I tell you I am perfectly happy with my situation?"

When she glanced around he had gone back to his place, but she felt no reassurance, especially when she had to force her eyes not to feast on him. He wanted her to marry for love, even if it was not himself. That was love speaking. And she wanted him to marry for love, because she loved him.

And they were both condemned to something much, much less.

# =13=

A BREAK WAS called for shade and lemonade. Everyone collapsed beneath the oak in shameless abandon. Lucy Frogmorton lowered her gaze from the horizon only when Rowanford sat beside her.

Amy frowned at this. She hadn't driven him off just to see him fall into Lucy's greedy paws. She looked at Clyta, who was laughing at something Lord Templemore had said to her, something slightly naughty, Amy would guess. It had the effect of making Clyta look magnificent. Relaxed among friends in the country, Clyta was at her best.

With determination, Amy sat beside the duke and was pleased to hear that Lucy was complaining about the lack of decorum. The duke did not look as if he enjoyed the topic, and he turned away readily enough when Amy broke into the conversation.

"I do hope you weren't offended over the horse, your grace," she said in her best demure manner. "I feel so touched that you wanted to take care of me, and it is a long time since I last rode a spirited animal."

He preened a little. "Not at all, Miss de Lacy. I will certainly know better another time. And you mustn't be 'your gracing' me as if we were strangers."

"You're very kind. I did used to be a good rider, but I was never as good as Clyta."

He looked over at Clyta as she had intended. "No, she's a wonderful horsewoman."

Clyta laughed again. Her heavy dark hair was escaping its pins and she was beginning to look wanton, but in this situation it might work to her advantage. "She's enjoying herself," Amy said softly, trying to keep his attention fixed to Clyta. "She much prefers the country to London."

"Oh," said the duke, his eyes fixed where Amy wanted them as if glued.

"It is her duty, I suppose, as a duke's granddaughter to do a Season," Amy persevered, feeling like the serpent in the Garden of Eden. "I'm sure she'll marry well, don't you think, Duke? I know any number of eligible men are already interested." She leaned closer to his ear. "Don't you think her very handsome?"

By some act of Providence, Chart chose that moment to tease his sister so she pounced on him for a minor tussle. Her hair came down completely and a great deal of her shapely legs was revealed before Chart realized this and established some control.

"My, my," said Rowanford in the tones of a man who has had a revelation.

"Oh dear," said Amy briskly, leaping to her feet. "If Chart's going to tease, I think we should go and rescue Clyta. Brothers can be horrible," she added, whose only brother had never given her that kind of trouble at all.

Like a puppet, the duke got to his feet and followed. Amy settled him by Clyta, then drew Chart off. When she looked back and saw Clyta laughing and joking with the duke without a trace of shyness, and Rowanford leaning closer, bewitched, she felt she had done a fine piece of work. It might not amount to anything but it was a start, and in the hedonistic atmosphere of Maiden Hall anything could happen.

She glanced back at Lucy and received a glare of dislike. She felt no ill will toward the young woman and would have tried a little matchmaking on her behalf if she could, but Lucy couldn't have Rowanford because Clyta wanted him, and she couldn't have Chart or Harry because they both deserved a warmer heart.

Amy wasn't aware that Lord Templemore had disappeared until he came back. "I have arranged a little entertainment," he said with a twinkle in his eyes.

Amy immediately felt alarm and anticipation. What now?

"Not the maze," said Lord Randal with a groan.

"The maze," said Lord Templemore.

"Do you really have a maze?" asked Clyta, bouncing to her feet, then leaning down to pull Rowanford up. Amy winced, but the duke didn't seem to mind at all.

"I really do. A genuine Elizabethan maze that took a devilish amount of work to shape up again. Come and see."

The ladies resumed their stockings and boots, but that was the only gesture toward resuming propriety before they walked around the house. Amy was pleased to see the duke staying close to Clyta. She wondered why Lord Randal had seemed so amused at the thought of the maze. It sounded interesting, but no more than that.

They were walking along a tall, dense box hedge when Lord Templemore stopped by a narrow gap. Amy realized the hedge was part of the maze. It was at least eight feet high and impenetrable and stretched quite a distance in either direction. The narrow gap led to a path between more dense hedges. Amy suddenly felt nervous.

"There are four entrances—or exits," said their host, "and a central square with some statues. I've left two prizes in the center, one for the first lady, one for the first gentleman. They are to be given to the partner of their choice." It was clear from the glint in his eye that he knew that could open some mischievous pathways.

"I think the ladies should go in first," he said. "Who will volunteer?"

Clyta stepped forward. "I will. But what if we can't find our way out?"

"Someone will rescue you before dark, I promise."

With a flitting, teasing look at the duke, Clyta slipped through the gap and moved out of sight. Rowanford made as if to follow, but Lord Templemore stopped him.

"On to the next entrance," he said and led the way. It was some distance to the corner, and then Amy could see the dimensions more clearly. "This is enormous," she said.

"Yes,"agreed Lord Templemore. "Are you game to go next?"

There seemed no point in refusing, so Amy slipped between the trimmed box and into the maze. The outer path went forward the length of the maze, cut by a number of gaps leading inward. Amy listened, but it was quiet now. She couldn't even hear the voices of the others. It was as if she were alone in the narrow green world, and she poked her head back out to assure herself that the real world was still there.

Then she stiffened her nerve and took the next gap.

Sometimes the paths became dead ends, sometimes they went in circles. She tried to carry some plan of where she had been but found it impossible. She encountered no one, and a fear that she was stuck in the maze began to grow in her. She imagined the others back at the house having tea and laughing at the joke they had played to trap her here.

She began to hurry, then run, plunging always through the first gap she came to. She heard a noise through the hedge. "Hello!" she cried. "Who's there?"

"Miss de Lacy?" It was Lucy Frogmorton. "Oh, this is horrible. How can I get to your side?"

Amy came to her senses. She wouldn't be as much of a ninny as Lucy. "I don't know," she called. "Don't worry. Just wander around. You'll either get out, or to the middle sooner or later."

"I want to get out now!" Lucy demanded.

"Scream then," recommended Amy and headed away from the voice. She didn't hear any screaming, so Lucy must have decided not to make a fool of herself. Amy took her own advice and wandered. If she began to feel trapped, she looked up at the blue sky. Whenever she heard a sound she called out, and she made contact with Clyta and Chart that way, though she never saw them.

She was amused to find small grottoes here and there in dead ends. They were furnished with benches and a certain amount of screening. In view of her host's rakish reputation she could imagine their purpose.

She found her mind dwelling on the kind of parties that had doubtless been held here in his bachelor days, with ladies and gentlemen finding and losing each other in these dark green passageways, feeling alone together here, apart from the world and all the burdens of responsibility and correct behavior.

She wondered if Lord Templemore wandered here with his wife to stop and share kisses in a secret corner. She could imagine it. It was perhaps improper to dwell on such things but she couldn't help it. She could imagine Lord Randal and Sophie enjoying the same pleasure.

There would be none of that for her. No teasing romps, no romantic trysts. Amy allowed her mind in a direction she had never permitted it before. She knew, in general terms, what marriage involved. She imagined her marriage bed when Sir Cedric joined her. He would kiss her, and then do what he had to do. She supposed he would enjoy it, for men apparently did, but it was hard to imagine any enjoyment for herself. It was equally hard to imagine Sir Cedric looking at her with the hunger she had seen in other eyes today.

Having opened her mind to these thoughts, they could not be shut out. She saw new dimensions to the world around her. She had thought Lord Templmore's gaze at his wife heated, but now she recognized hunger. It was decently controlled by maturity, civilization, and, she supposed, the expectation of satisfaction, but it was hunger all the same. She remembered the way Sophie had said, "Married life is so exhausting," and the gleam in her husband's eye. Hunger again.

And maybe there had been just a little hunger in Rowanford's eyes when he looked at Clyta. Amy certainly hoped so.

It had been there in Harry's and, she suspected, in her own. She sighed. Was she to go hungry all her life?

She turned a corner and came face to face with Harry.

"Ah, another human being," he said lightly, but his eyes were hungry.

Amy swallowed. "Just what I was thinking."

It was silent and shadowed and cool. She walked toward him and put her hands on his broad shoulders. "I'd like you please to kiss me, just once."

His arms came to rest at her waist, and his breathing was suddenly unsteady. "Why just once?"

She rested her head against his warm shoulder and heard the pounding of his heart. She watched as her hand slid down his damp neck to play among the curls on his chest. "Well, maybe twice."

His hand came up to cover hers against his skin, holding it still for a moment. Then he grasped it, moved apart from her, and set off back the way he had come, pulling her behind him.

"Where are we going?" she demanded. "Don't you want to kiss me?"

"Yes, I want to kiss you," he said and turned a corner that led to a grotto. He sat on the bench and drew her down beside him. His eyes were dark and dangerous, and Amy knew she was in peril, delicious peril.

He drew her against him with a relentless arm, guided her head with his other hand, and kissed her. It was not the gentle, questing kiss they had shared before, but hotly demanding and not a little angry. Amy surrendered to it. She, too, was hungry and angry and hot.

She pressed herself closer and held him tighter, sliding her hands beneath his shirt to feel his heated skin. She tasted him and swirled within a mad, heated passion, a hunger that was not appeased but grew and grew.

"God," he groaned and tore his lips from hers.

Amy made a faint protest, then came to herself and stared at him, dazed. She had somehow come to be on his lap, and his shirt looked as if she had half torn it off his body. "I'm terribly hard on buttons," she wailed and burst into tears.

He held her and stroked her and murmured to her. He

held her tight and close as no one had held her before. Amy wept for Stonycourt, which would never be as it once was; for Beryl who would only be an aunt, never a mother; for Jassy who would not marry well; for Jasper who wouldn't have a string of hunters and host the Belvoir; and for herself who wouldn't have any joy either because she wouldn't be happy if none of the others could be.

The sobs faded to gulps and then to numb silence. Amy clung close, filling her senses with the feel of his body and the scent of his skin, something to take with her and remember.

"You take buttons very seriously," he said shakily. His hand cradled her head, his fingers sending a message of comfort.

Amy sniffed. "You have to when you're poor."

He pushed her away. "There's no need for you to be poor, Amy. I can take care of you."

Amy shook her head. "Can you provide dowries for Jassy and Beryl?"

"Something, at least."

"Something isn't enough." She looked up at him. "I don't have a dowry, you know."

"I guessed. It doesn't matter." He looked impatient. "Isn't it a bit arrogant for you assume that your sisters can't find love without money to sweeten the pot?"

Amy pushed away sharply. "That's a horrid thing to say!"

"It's what you're saying."

"No it isn't!" She jumped off his lap entirely. "It's just that that's the way of the world. At least they need decent clothes."

"I fell in love with you in a blanket."

Amy's anger escaped her. "Oh, don't."

"Don't what?"

"Don't say you love me."

"But I do."

"So do I." She clapped her hand over her mouth to call back the error.

He grasped her shoulders and pulled her closer. "Then you cannot marry anyone else."

"I love my family, too."

"Do they love you?" he asked in exasperation.

"Of course they do!"

"Then they won't want you to marry where you don't love, Amy. Why are you doing this?"

"They won't know. They *mustn't* know."

"Of course they'll know." He gave her a little shake. "Have some sense!"

"Stop shouting at me!"

"I feel like strangling you! If I had any sense I'd take you here and now in this damned bower and then you'd *have* to marry me."

They stared at one another and Amy knew it was temptation which wove through the heated air. She'd have to marry him, and she wanted him, now. Hunger. She hadn't recognized it before.

She backed away.

"Amy," he said and held out a hand.

She turned and fled.

She did not look, just ran, gasping. She collided with a hard body. Hands grasped and steadied her.

"Miss de Lacy," said Lord Randal. "Are you all right?"

Amy collapsed against him, heart thudding. "No."

He held her for a moment, then pushed her gently away so he could look at her. He was very sober for one so lighthearted. "What has happened?"

Amy took a deep breath. She knew what he thought. "If I said Harry and I had . . . committed an indiscretion, you'd say we had to get married, wouldn't you?"

"The world would."

"You wouldn't?"

His earlier somberness had gone and he looked, if anything, amused. "It would depend, I suppose, on the indiscretion, the consequences, and the feelings you share."

She might have known she'd get no sane answers from these people. They were all mad. Amy turned away. "Nothing happened," she said flatly.

"That is a lie."

She turned sharply, guiltily. "What do you mean?"

He just smiled, shook his head, and gently rearranged her bodice. "Let me escort you out of here."

She went willingly. Perhaps once out of the strange world of narrow green paths she could find sanity again.

In a little while he said, "This wasn't planned, Miss de Lacy."

"What wasn't?"

"Today. I admit we connived a little to bring you and Harry together at the ball. We all thought you'd both be better to get one another out of your systems. But today, well it was Rowanford's idea to invite you, and he was supported by Clyta. Now I think I see why. I noted the way you've tried to help her. Thank you."

"She's my friend. She'd do as much for me."

"We all would," he said gently.

Amy looked at him in surprise and swallowed tears. It was all too much. "I am an unscrupulous fortune hunter, Lord Randal. Your kindness is misguided."

He smiled with amazing sweetness. "I don't think so."

They had reached an exit, and they passed out into open spaces and clean air. Amy shuddered as reality invaded and cooled her senses, opening the way for the enormity of what had happened. Lady Templemore was nearby and she hurried over.

Lord Randal spoke first. "I think Miss de Lacy would appreciate returning to the house, Emily, for some peace and a cup of tea."

"Of course. Miss Frogmorton is already there with a cool cloth on her head. The maze does not usually have such a dramatic effect."

"Are the others still inside?" he asked.

"I think so."

"Then I had best go and find Sophie. I'm sure the rest will manage with ease."

"Do you imply Sophie will be having the vapors?" queried Lady Templemore skeptically.

"Of course not," he said with a smile. "I just miss her."

With that he disappeared back into the maze, and Amy followed her hostess toward the house.

"You look a little pale, dear. I do hope it wasn't the maze. It can upset some people. I confess at first I found it strange, but now I like it. It's like entering a separate world."

"Yes, it is," said Amy, adding to herself, An extremely dangerous one.

Amy took tea with Lucy and Lady Templemore, and the others gradually drifted in to join them. Everyone else seemed to have had a merry time, and Clyta and the duke had clearly had some satisfactory encounter there. They both looked dazed but happy. Clyta had found the ladies' prize—a silver fob—and given it to Rowanford without hesitation.

Harry came in last. He had already resumed proper dress and looked sober. He had found the gentlemen's prize, perhaps because none of the others had bothered to look. He considered the ladies thoughtfully, then presented it to his hostess.

She unwrapped the small package to reveal a gold frog brooch with green eyes, which were presumably emeralds. It was a valuable piece but very ugly.

Lady Templemore laughed at her husband. "What a wonderful way of trying to get rid of it, Ver, but you see, it simply won't go away."

"We'll try again," he said with a grin. He explained, "It was given Emily by an eccentric Italian acquaintance of mine, and she's afraid she'll give birth to frogs if she wears it."

The lady protested and there was considerable banter. Lucy looked as if she'd like to faint, and Amy was shocked at the casual way Lord Templemore referred to his wife's condition. No one else appeared to be.

Sophie said, "I think you should give the frog to Lucy."

Everyone looked at her for an explanation. "It would suit her—because of her name, of course," she added blithely. "And she'd be doing the world a favor. Bad enough having little Verderans without them having green skin and bulging eyes."

Lucy took the piece in a daze, clearly at a loss, and then they all prepared to depart.

Lord Templemore offered Amy another mount but she refused. The fewer high spirits there were today the better.

The ride home was uneventful. Everyone was content with a leisurely pace, satiated almost with excitement. The duke rode happily with Clyta, but the other couples were arranged for tact. Amy was partnered with Chart, who kept conversation light and impersonal, Sophie rode with Harry, and Lord Randal was using his considerable charm to soothe Lucy Frogmorton before she was returned to her mama.

Amy saw Harry look back at her with intensity once or twice, but he made no move to speak to her.

When they arrived back in New Street, however, it was he who came to assist Amy from her horse.

He kept his hands on her waist a moment longer than necessary. "I meant what I said."

"So did I. Please don't make things more difficult for me."

"So you admit they are difficult."

Amy pulled herself out of his hands and summoned a smile for the whole company as she thanked them. Then there was only the matter of giving a light account of her day to Nell and her aunt before she could find refuge in her room.

It seemed as if she had come out of a dream. It couldn't have been real—the barefoot romping, the passion, the kiss. But one thing remained. She did not want an old man in her bed.

Amy claimed to have developed a headache from too much sun and kept to her room the next day. Both Lord and Lady Randal, and Harry Crisp came to call on her separately and were sent away.

Amy tussled with what was right.

She was quite certain that she must not marry Harry. The pleasure to be found in that was too great when there would be so little for her family. But would it be a better thing for them all to suffer the straightened circumstances which they deserved—by inheritance if not from personal responsibility—or for her to marry Sir Cedric?

Amy was still willing to marry Sir Cedric and do her best to make him a good wife, but she knew now what she would be missing and how little she had to offer. Such an old man would not want passion, of course, but he would expect some warmth. Did she have that for him?

And, of course, Amy would have to give him what devotion she could under the eyes of his chilly son and saddened daughter-in-law, even as she grabbed as much of his money as she could get her hands on so it would all be worthwhile.

Amy's headache became a grim reality.

# ═14═

SHE KEPT TO HER room the next day, too. Nell and Lizzie both fussed over her and discussed whether to send for the doctor. Amy assured them that was not necessary.

"Sir Cedric is expected back today," said Nell. "Will you not want to see him?"

"No," said Amy, a little more forcefully than she intended. "I mean . . . I really wouldn't be good company today. Apologize for me, please."

Lizzie came up with a tea tray in the afternoon and coaxed Amy into taking a little. "Been overdoing it, I suppose. But you must get your looks back before Sir Cedric cools down, dear. Most anxious to see you, he was. He seemed to want someone to go for a drive with him, so Nell went."

Get her looks back. Amy sat up and studied her reflection in the mirror. Good heavens, her beauty was fading. It was the pallor and the dark smudges beneath her eyes which were doing it. Perhaps she wouldn't have any choice as to whether to remain a spinster or not.

"And no sign of that duke," said Lizzie, "so it will have to be the banker, I suppose."

"If the worst comes to the worst," said Amy, "it won't be so bad to carry on as we were. In just a few years we'll be able to live in modest comfort."

"What!" exclaimed Lizzie. "Back at Stonycourt, living on potatoes, mutton, and chamomile tea. You must be mad!"

Amy retreated. "It's just that he hasn't offered for me, Aunt Lizzie, and there doesn't seem to be anyone else."

"How can he offer for you if you mope up here? Drink your tea and get well." When she left with the tray she said, "Oh, that Mr. Crisp was here again. Some people won't be put off, will they? He left something for you. I'll have the footman bring it up."

Amy found her energy had returned with a jolt and sat up in bed. The footman, escorted by Aunt Lizzie, carried in a medium-sized box and placed it on the bed. When he had gone Amy opened it with some anxiety. He had said he intended to woo her. What on earth would it be?

The crate contained an item swathed in cloth and surrounded by padding. When the bundled object was unwrapped it proved to be Lady Jane.

"Pretty," said Lizzie as Amy lifted it out gently. "Though what he thinks he's about sending you gifts I don't know. I would have thought you'd shown him what you thought of him clearly enough."

Amy ignored this and turned the key. The music started, the sweet tinkling tune carrying her straight back to Coppice Farm. Lady Jane turned her head gracefully, then began to lift her leg. There was a *ping* and the leg fell limp again, though the music played on.

"Why, it doesn't even work!" exclaimed Lizzie. "I'll have Simon come and get it. Mr. Crisp can have his gift straight back."

"No," said Amy. "It's pretty and the music box works." With a sniff, Lizzie left.

When she was alone Amy picked up the note that had been in the box and opened it. She had never seen his handwriting before. It was dark and a little wild.

*Darling Amy,*
*I hope you will take Lady Jane. She means a lot to both of us, as a memory of that time in my kitchen with your clothes abandoned in the corner and us sharing such delights. Of course, I hope we will one day be reunited, you, me, and Lady Jane.*

*I cannot doubt that, when I think of our passion yes-terday. I remember you throwing off your stockings, so eager were you. My skin still bears the marks of your nails, my mind the memory of your desire.*

*You are the only one I desire. I long to see you nestled in my blanket once again.*

*Harry*

After a shocked moment, Amy collapsed in laughter. The cunning rogue. Not an untrue word in it and if anyone saw it she'd be at the altar with him in the twinkling of an eye. There was more on the back.

*Lady Jane is, I'm afraid, irreparable. I still think her worthy of care. Not everything can be put back together as it was.*

*Your loving Harry*

That was a direct reference to her purpose, but he was wrong. Many things could be put right, and as he had proved with the automaton, it was often worth the effort.

Amy looked at the note. She should destroy it, but the temptation was very strong to leave it around and let fate take its course. Aunt Lizzie was certainly not above reading someone else's correspondence. In the end she slipped it between the pages of her book. It was Adam Smith's *The Wealth of Nations,* and she didn't think Lizzie would pick that up.

What on earth would he try next? She couldn't let him get away with this. She had to make her own decisions and stick to them.

Amy got out of bed and went to the window. Was she going to marry Sir Cedric or not?

Presumably he was mainly interested in her beauty, since they had so little else in common. She could offer him that, as long as she didn't allow misery to fade it. It would be an honest bargain—youth and beauty for money.

That sounded despicable.

Amy straightened her shoulders. It was the way of the

world. The family had spent so much money to send her to London that it would be wicked to turn her back on triumph when it was to hand. Moreover, she ruthlessly acknowledged that she had no real expectation of going back home to live in poverty. If she didn't marry Sir Cedric, she would doubtless be won over by Harry one of these days. She would end up with everything she had ever wanted, while her family had nothing.

Amy resolutely spent an hour walking in the garden to bring some color to her cheeks, but she made sure she was to be denied to all callers. She could not bear to see Harry. She went down to dinner that night.

Nell seemed to be in a fidgety mood, and chattered of this and that. She did not mention her drive with Sir Cedric, so nothing of significance could have been said. Anyway, Amy supposed he would approach Aunt Lizzie for permission to pay his addresses, not Nell.

"Tell me, Amy," said Nell, who had only picked at her roast chicken, "what of the duke? He seemed a very charming young man."

"He's pleasant as dukes go," said Amy. "I hope I've tied him up with Clyta Ashby. She's madly in love with him."

"Oh," said Nell. "I thought you would make a lovely duchess."

"Indeed she would," said Lizzie. "It would have been a triumph to warm her mother's heart. But no, she has to push him off on her friend and settle for a mere knight." She helped herself to more peas.

"Oh dear," said Nell faintly, then she jumped to her feet. "Look at the time. I am expected at Fanny Bamford's. I did promise to go early and help with her soirée. She always worries so. Do please excuse me."

"I must say," said Lizzie staring at the door, "Nell is behaving most strangely. She used to be a very sensible woman."

Amy smiled. "I think she's in love, Aunt."

"In love? Nonsense. Not at her age. Are you finished? Ring for the sweet. It's apricot soufflé."

Amy did as she was requested, reflecting that she would

once have thought Nell too old for love, but no longer. The hunger that was love had nothing to do with age.

By the next day Amy had regained some of her detachment and all of her resolve. If Sir Cedric truly wished to marry her, she would agree. She would be honest, though. She would tell him that she could offer nothing but friendship and genuine regard. After some consideration she decided she wouldn't tell him she loved another; he would doubtless be as romantical as all the rest and insist that she sacrifice all for love.

She would also explain the financial commitment she required from him. If after all this he still wanted her, she would accept.

Amy sat in her room, awaiting the news that he had called, aware of a secret hope that all her cavils and demands would be too much for him.

The ormolu clock ticked away the afternoon. What if he didn't come? If he truly wanted to see her, he would come.

Amy thought she heard something and went to her window. His carriage!

She rushed to the mirror and checked her appearance. She was improved. Not in full bloom, but well enough, surely, and the blue sprig muslin she was wearing was her most becoming. She generally maided herself, but today she had requested Nell's maid to weave some ribbons through her curls, and the effect was pleasing.

Amy went to the door and hovered, waiting for the summons, hands clasped anxiously.

The clock ticked on. What was happening?

Of course, he would have asked to speak to Aunt Lizzie first. But Aunt Lizzie had gone to the British Museum with a friend, Mrs. Fellows. Perhaps he was speaking to Nell instead.

Amy paced the room, glancing at the monotonous clock. It must have been quite twenty minutes.

She stopped dead. What if the foolish maid had forgotten that she was home to Sir Cedric? Amy hadn't seen

Nell to tell her she was receiving guests. Sir Cedric could this very minute be leaving.

Amy couldn't bear another day of this waiting. She ran out into the corridor and down the stairs. She slowed in relief when she saw the empty hall. At least he wasn't leaving yet.

The drawing room was open; the room was empty. They must be in the morning room.

Amy hesitated. She didn't want to barge in like an overeager hussy, but it wouldn't take this long for Nell to give him permission to make his offer. They must think she was still unwell.

Amy walked up to the door. She raised her hand to knock, but that was silly. This was a public room. She turned the handle, walked in, and stopped dead.

The couple didn't notice her for a moment, which wasn't surprising since Nell was on Sir Cedric's lap and they were kissing with passionate abandon. Perhaps Amy made a sound, for they broke apart and stared at her with horror.

In a flash Nell was up and rearranging her gown. Sir Cedric was on his feet twitching at his disarranged cravat.

Amy backed away.

"Amy, dear, don't go," said Nell. "Let us explain."

"There's nothing to explain," said Amy numbly. "I'm . . . I'm very happy for you. I'm sorry I interrupted."

Nell grasped her hand and wouldn't let her flee. "You must come and talk, dear. We can't pretend nothing has happened here. Cedric and I have been feeling dreadful ever since we realized."

Amy found herself sitting down, with Nell and Sir Cedric facing her like guilty children. "Really," she said. "It's nothing to do with me."

"Yes it is," said Sir Cedric firmly, for all that he looked like a raw stripling. "I paid you particular attentions, Miss de Lacy. I was greatly attracted to your beauty, but also by your inner qualities. You have courage, honesty, and wit. I thought we could make a comfortable match of it to both our benefits." He looked to his side and took Nell's hand in his. "My feelings for Nell took me quite by surprise."

Amy was aware that this was a disaster, but she couldn't help delight in their love. "I'm glad," she said. "I truly am."

Nell smiled mistily. "Oh, Amy. You really are amazing. You mean it, don't you?"

"Yes. You both deserve to love and be loved. Everyone does." Amy sighed and rose. "It is probably time for Lizzie and I to return home."

"Lizzie has been offered a home with a friend, Dorothy Fellows,"said Nell apologetically. "I think she will prefer to stay in London."

Amy felt as if this was abandonment, which was ridiculous. "Well, that's one less mouth to feed," she said.

She tried to make the door again, but Sir Cedric put himself between her and it. "Miss de Lacy—Amy—I will not let you run away. There are matters to be discussed. Though there is no longer any question of a marriage between us, I do feel very fond of you, as if you were a daughter. I have considered how best to help you—"

"No!" said Amy. "You must not. We are not a charity case."

"You cannot refuse to let me help you."

"I can and do. We will manage for ourselves."

"My dear child, you were willing to sacrifice yourself—for that is what it amounted to—for the sake of your family. Can you not let go of a scrap of your pride?"

Amy was trying to find an answer to this when a commotion erupted outside. "That sounds like Jasper," Amy said in amazement and headed for the door. This time no one stopped her.

Nell's hall was full of people.

"Amy!" cried Jassy, running into her arms. "Isn't this a wonderful surprise?"

Amy hugged her younger sister and looked over at a smiling Beryl. A Beryl who was arm in arm with a frowning Mr. Staverley.

"What on earth has happened?" Amy asked.

"We've come to London for the Season," Jasper announced, then looked over Amy's shoulder. "Good afternoon, ma'am, sir. Sorry for the disturbance. Girls are always a bit overly excitable."

Reminded of her manners, a dazed Amy introduced her family to Nell and Sir Cedric. She still didn't understand why Mr. Staverley was here, especially as he looked so cross about it. "But you can't stay here," she told everyone. "Mrs. Claybury doesn't have room."

There was a gabble of explanation, which Amy could not follow, then Nell's voice cut through. "That is unfortunately true, but at least you must all come in for tea." Within moments everyone was settled in the drawing room and the tea tray had been ordered.

"Now," said Amy. "Will someone please explain what you're up to. This is madness. Where are you all to stay?"

"Owen's hired a house," declared Jasper. "Montague Street. Very handsome."

"But you can't stay there with him," Amy said blankly.

"Can," said Staverley. "Though we're in a hotel for tonight. Your sister and me, we're to be married. Tomorrow. Special license. Wanted to do it back home but she wouldn't hear of it without her favorite sister, so here we are. Honeymoon in London. Bound to be plenty of excitement for the younger ones with the victory celebrations." By the end of this speech, his frown had lifted a little and he merely looked flustered. He took Beryl's hand and they smiled at each other. For the first time, Amy noticed the handsome diamond on her sister's hand.

Amy was speechless. She heard Sir Cedric and Nell say all that was proper and tried to summon the right words herself, but Beryl was sacrificing herself because Amy had failed.

"Amy, dear, aren't you happy for me?"

Beryl had come to sit beside her. "Are you happy?" Amy asked.

Beryl smiled. "Of course I am, dearest. You don't mind, do you? I know you didn't take a great liking to Owen, but I'm sure you'll come to see his qualities as I do."

"Well, he's rich," said Amy.

"Amy, dear," said Beryl with a slight frown, "you know I would never marry for money alone. Owen and I are very fond of each other. Very fond." Beryl looked over at monkeyish Owen Staverley with warm devotion. He caught her eye and looked away, reddening. Hunger.

Amy became aware her mouth was hanging open and closed it.

"You mustn't mind his manner," Beryl said quietly. "He's just shy, you see, and hides it with a frown. He feels ill at ease until he knows people well. But he's the soul of generosity. He's settled a handsome amount on Jassy and put money into the estate, so by the time Jasper achieves his majority the estate should be debt free."

"He must have put in a great deal of money," said Amy, startled.

"Yes, but he said it was made easier because someone had recently done something with the debts. I don't understand it, but you may. They've been bought up, I think, and the interest reduced to a mere nothing. Perhaps it was something Uncle Cuthbert arranged."

Amy looked over at Sir Cedric, who was clearly attending to this conversation. He looked rueful and winked.

Her stunned amazement was beginning to fade, and facts were beginning to settle and sort in her mind. There was a chance that it was all going to be all right. Could she dare believe it?

More arrivals. Amy looked up to see Harry, Randal, and Sophie at the door. Numbly awaiting what was to come next, Amy made a fresh round of introductions. Nell ordered more cups and tea.

Randal and Sophie sat. Harry remained standing.

"I have come," he said loudly, "to ask Miss de Lacy to marry me."

"You can't," said Amy pleasantly. "She's going to marry Mr. Staverley."

Harry looked startled, but then laughed. "I have come to ask Miss Amethyst de Lacy to marry me. Will you Amy?"

Amy considered him. "I would have thought after last time that you'd have realized I don't much care for such blunt proposals."

"After last time," he said bluntly, "and all that's gone in between, I'm not sure it's worth making a long speech of it."

He seemed quite unconscious of their fascinated audience. Not so Amy, particularly if he intended a review of their encounters. She stood. "Perhaps we can continue this discussion in private."

He stopped her before she reached the door and wrapped an imprisoning arm around her. "Oh no, I may need witnesses."

"What on earth are you talking about?" But Amy relaxed against his body and laid her head on his shoulder.

He leaned close to her ear, which was enough in itself to make her begin to lose her hold on her senses. "That note should have given you a hint," he whispered. "I'll stop at nothing, wench. It's up my sleeve."

"What is?" she murmured, fighting giggles. Everyone was staring at them as if they'd gone mad.

"Your shift," he whispered, warm and soft against her ear. "Shall I pull it out and wave it before the company, or do you surrender gracefully?"

Amy was very tempted to call his bluff. When had she become such a wicked, reckless woman? But she surrendered, if not very gracefully. "I'll probably accept you," she said clearly, "if you mange to make a handsome proposal."

He looked startled, then blindingly happy. She realized that he knew nothing of what had transpired today but had truly come to force her hand by any means possible.

He went dramatically to one knee. "My dearest Amethyst, precious jewel of my heart, I can imagine no joy in life if you are not by my side. In my eyes you are perfect. I adore you. Give me the right to love and cherish you forever."

He was acting the fool, but his eyes told her every exaggerated word was true.

Amy gave her hand and drew him to his feet, fighting tears. "I think you should know I would have married Sir Cedric if he'd asked me. He's going to marry Nell instead."

"Congratulations, sir," said Harry to the banker. "No you wouldn't," he said to Amy. "Why do you think I came armed?"

"You really would?" she asked.

"I really would. That's why I brought Randal. He'd force us to the altar if no one else did."

"I haven't the faintest idea what he's talking about," said Randal. "But I would point out that you haven't answered, Amy, and the tea tray is behind you."

Amy and Harry stepped out of the doorway to allow the maid to bring in the tea.

"Well?" said Harry.

"I'm scared," said Amy.

"What on earth of? Of me?"

"No, no, never of you. I'm scared this will all be a dream."

He gathered her into his arms, despite the crowded room. "I'll make it a dream that will last your whole life long. Say yes, darling."

"Yes, darling."

As Harry kissed Amy, Beryl beamed at her betrothed and said, "Do you know, Owen, dear, you are joining the most fortunate family in the world."

# Avon Regency Romance

## Kasey Michaels

THE CHAOTIC MISS CRISPINO
76300-1/$3.99 US/$4.99 Can

THE DUBIOUS MISS DALRYMPLE
89908-6/$2.95 US/$3.50 Can

THE HAUNTED MISS HAMPSHIRE
76301-X/$3.99 US/$4.99 Can

## Loretta Chase

THE ENGLISH WITCH
70660-1/$2.95 US/$3.50 Can

ISABELLA
70597-4/$2.95 US/$3.95 Can

KNAVES' WAGER
71363-2/$3.95 US/$4.95 Can

THE SANDALWOOD PRINCESS
71455-8/$3.99 US/$4.99 Can

THE VISCOUNT VAGABOND
70836-1/$2.95 US/$3.50 Can

## Jo Beverley

EMILY AND THE DARK ANGEL
71555-4/$3.99 US/$4.99 Can

THE STANFORTH SECRETS
71438-8/$3.99 US/$4.99 Can

# Avon Romantic Treasures

*Unforgettable, enthralling love stories,*
*sparkling with passion and adventure*
*from Romance's bestselling authors*

FIRE ON THE WIND *by Barbara Dawson Smith*
76274-9/$4.50 US/$5.50 Can

DANCE OF DECEPTION *by Suzannah Davis*
76128-9/$4.50 US/$5.50 Can

ONLY IN YOUR ARMS *by Lisa Kleypas*
76150-5/$4.50 US/$5.50 Can

LADY LEGEND *by Deborah Camp*
76735-X/$4.50 US/$5.50 Can

RAINBOWS AND RAPTURE *by Rebecca Paisley*
76565-9/$4.50 US/$5.50 Can

AWAKEN MY FIRE *by Jennifer Horsman*
76701-5/$4.50 US/$5.50 Can

ONLY BY YOUR TOUCH *by Stella Cameron*
76606-X/$4.50 US/$5.50 Can

# The WONDER of WOODIWISS

continues with the upcoming publication of
her newest novel in trade paperback—

## FOREVER IN YOUR EMBRACE

☐ #89818-7

$12.50 U.S. ($15.00 Canada)

### THE FLAME AND THE FLOWER

☐ #00525-5

$5.99 U.S. ($6.99 Canada)

### THE WOLF AND THE DOVE

☐ #00778-9

$5.99 U.S. ($6.99 Canada)

### SHANNA

☐ #38588-0

$5.99 U.S. ($6.99 Canada)

### ASHES IN THE WIND

☐ #76984-0

$5.99 U.S. ($6.99 Canada)

### A ROSE IN WINTER

☐ #84400-1

$5.99 U.S. ($6.99 Canada)

### COME LOVE A STRANGER

☐ #89936-1

$5.99 U.S. ($6.99 Canada)

### SO WORTHY MY LOVE

☐ #76148-3

$5.95 U.S. ($6.95 Canada)

# The Incomparable

# ELIZABETH LOWELL

## "Lowell is great!"
## Johanna Lindsey

### ONLY YOU

76340-0/$4.99 US/$5.99 Can

"For smoldering sensuality and exceptional storytelling,
Elizabeth Lowell is incomparable."

Kathe Robin, *Romantic Times*

### ONLY MINE

76339-7/$4.99 US/$5.99 Can

"Elizabeth Lowell is a law unto herself
in the world of romance."

Amanda Quick, author of SCANDAL

### ONLY HIS

76338-9/$4.95 US/$5.95 Can

Like the land, he was wild, exciting…and dangerous
and he vowed she would be only his.

# Avon Romances—
## *the best in exceptional authors and unforgettable novels!*

**WARRIOR DREAMS**   Kathleen Harrington
76581-0/$4.50 US/$5.50 Can

**MY CHERISHED ENEMY**   Samantha James
76692-2/$4.50 US/$5.50 Can

**CHEROKEE SUNDOWN**   Genell Dellin
76716-3/$4.50 US/$5.50 Can

**DESERT ROGUE**   Suzanne Simmons
76578-0/$4.50 US/$5.50 Can

**DEVIL'S DELIGHT**   DeLoras Scott
76343-5/$4.50 US/$5.50 Can

**RENEGADE LADY**   Sonya Birmingham
76765-1/$4.50 US/$5.50 Can

**LORD OF MY HEART**   Jo Beverley
76784-8/$4.50 US/$5.50 Can

**BLUE MOON BAYOU**   Katherine Compton
76412-1/$4.50 US/$5.50 Can

### *Coming Soon*

**SILVER FLAME**   Hannah Howell
76504-7/$4.50 US/$5.50 Can

**TAMING KATE**   Eugenia Riley
76475-X/$4.50 US/$5.50 Can

# 1 Out Of 5 Women Can't Read.

# 1 Out Of 5 Women Can't Read.

# 1 Out Of 5 Women Can't Read.

# 1 Xvz Xv 5 Xwywv Xvy'z Xvyz.

# 1 Out Of 5 Women Can't Read.

*As painful as it is to believe, it's true. And it's time we all did something to help. Coors has committed $40 million to fight illiteracy in America. We hope you'll join our efforts by volunteering your time. Giving just a few hours a week to your local literacy center can help teach a woman to read. For more information on literacy volunteering, call* **1-800-626-4601.**

LITERACY. PASS IT ON.